THE PRESIDENT'S

GIRLFRIEND

MALLORY

MONROE

c2011

***

AUSTIN BROOK PUBLISHING

MORE INTERRACIAL ROMANCE

FROM BESTSELLING AUTHOR

MALLORY MONROE:

MOB BOSS 2:

THE HEART OF THE MATTER

ROMANCING THE MOB BOSS

ROMANCING HER PROTECTOR

ROMANCING THE BULLDOG

IF YOU WANTED THE MOON

MALLORY MONROE

INTERRACIAL ROMANCE
FROM
BESTSELLING AUTHOR
KATHERINE CACHITORIE:

LOVING THE HEAD MAN

SOME CAME DESPERATE: A LOVE SAGA

WHEN WE GET MARRIED

ALSO
FAN FAVORITE
INTERRACIAL ROMANCE:

A SPECIAL RELATIONSHIP
YVONNE THOMAS

AND

BACK TO HONOR:
A REGGIE REYNOLDS
ROMANTIC MYSTERY
JT WATSON

COMING SOON
FROM
AUSTIN BROOK PUBLISHING

MORE INTERRACIAL ROMANCE
FROM
MALLORY MONROE:

THE PRESIDENT'S GIRLFRIEND 2:
HIS WOMEN AND HIS WIFE

AND

MOB BOSS 3:
ROMANCING TOMMY GABRINI

ALSO
AUSTIN BROOK PUBLISHING PRESENTS
ROMANTIC FICTION
FROM
AWARD-WINNING AND
BESTSELLING AUTHOR

TERESA MCCLAIN-WATSON

AFTER WHAT YOU DID
AND
STAY IN MY CORNER

Visit
**for more information
on all romance titles**

ONE

TEN YEARS EARLIER

The cab stopped in front of the Embassy-Grand Hotel in Miami Beach and Dutch Harber stepped out and walked inside. It had been a long day of meetings and more meetings and his body was near exhaustion. But the idea of going to bed alone, in that lonely hotel room not unlike all of those other lonely hotel rooms he'd had to endure since taking over the southern division of his father's company, was so unappealing to him that it was downright intolerable.

That was why, within seconds of entering the room, he exited back out. Back on the elevator to the lobby, back into the lobby through the east end colonnade, across the colonnade enclosed with gardens and fountains, and into the hotel's lounge.

It was rather rowdy for such a swanky lounge, but when he took a seat at a back booth and ordered himself a drink, he realized why. A group of young, raucous conventioneers were at a large table near his booth, laughing and talking and drinking like there was no tomorrow.

It was a large group, with the men displaying the kind of loud exuberance that equal doses of success and arrogance often bred, and the women, all tall, mostly blonde and thin as rails, solicitous to the men to a point that seemed almost calculating.

Except for one woman, Dutch noticed, the only African-American in the group. Nothing blonde or thin or solicitous about her. She, in fact, unlike the other females, seemed to exhibit that superior air the males displayed, rather than that coquettish submissiveness displayed by the females at the table. Although she appeared far too young to be their boss, and none of the females were kowtowing to her, she, unlike them, wasn't kowtowing to any of the males.

As the waiter returned with his drink, Dutch found himself watching her more closely. She was an interesting one, that lady. Had a style all her own. And forget thin and boyish-looking. She was voluptuous, with that curvaceous, oh-so-feminine body that always turned Dutch on. She wore a pale pink cocktail dress that crisscrossed at her cleavage, highlighting for all to see two ripe, plump breasts that, as soon as Dutch's eyes caught full sight of them, caused his penis to give a little thump.

And her face, now that was her money shot, he thought. Big, gorgeous eyes, a small, narrow nose, full lips that curled to a peak at the middle and trailed down in a soft sweep at the sides. And all of it put together on deep-toned, dark brown skin that seemed so smooth, so velvety rich that Dutch could imagine the warm, soft feel of it in his very capable hands.

Oddly enough, it wasn't anything remarkably beautiful about her that drew his interest, but it was more because she had that *something about her* special attraction that seemed to transcend mere handsomeness. And that look about her, that above-the-fray, uncompromising look that could just as easily be construed as arrogance as much as confidence and independence.   Seemed to him a self-assured female like her would be a tough sell in that group of superficial, spray-tanned Barbie and Ken dolls, but who was he to judge?   Maybe she was just as superficial as they were, but was better at camouflaging it.

He asked for and received a copy of the Wall Street Journal, flapped it open to the daily stock market report, and crossed his legs. But every time he tried to read any article, he kept getting interrupted by bursts of laughter from the conventioneers. It became so bad that even the Maitre d attempted to rescue him.

"Perhaps you'll feel more comfortable at a table in a different section, sir," he had suggested. But Dutch had declined. Let kids by kids, he always believed. He certainly was when he was their age.

He snorted at the way he phrased that. He'd only just turned thirty-three himself, but was talking as if he was his father's age. Certainly his father's poor health changed him, forcing him to take on more and more of the day to day operations of the family's numerous business interests, and the fact that his fiancée had died in a plane crash a little less than a year ago, would make any young man old. And although the loud conventioneers seemed to all be in their twenties, and was therefore not that much younger than he, youthful exuberance was about as foreign to him now as this new life of responsibility on top of responsibility was familiar.

As he buried his head in his newspaper and eventually learned to live with the noise, he suddenly felt the presence of someone standing at his booth. When he looked up, that same young lady he was observing earlier, the black woman, was right in front of him.

"Hi," she said in a soft, warm voice that reminded him of those smoky-voiced jazz singers his father used to love to listen to when Dutch was a kid.

"Hello," he replied, removing his reading glasses.

"Mind if I join you?"

Dutch's eyes, as if by reflex, trailed down to her breasts. "Not at all," he said. "Have a seat." He stood up slightly as she sat down.

"We're disturbing you, aren't we?"

"Why would you think that?" he asked, sitting back down.

"Because every time a roar goes up from our table, you cringe."

Dutch smiled. "Do I really?"

"You really do. And I mean it's very obvious." She extended her hand. "I'm Gina. Well, Regina, actually, but everybody calls me Gina."

Dutch removed his glasses from his right hand and shook hers. "Nice to meet you, Gina. I'm Walter."

"Whoa, you don't look like a Walter."

"Everybody calls me Dutch."

Gina smiled a smile so white and bright and inviting that Dutch found himself mesmerized by her mouth. "That's more like it then," she said with a playful head bob, a bob that caused her breasts to shake ever so slightly but, in so shaking, caused his penis to thump yet again.

"Are you from around these parts, Gina?" he asked her, oddly pleased to have her in his booth.

"Not hardly," she said. "I'm a Jersey girl. From Newark. What about you?"

"Boston."

"Boston, Mass. A businessman?"

"Now how did you guess?"

"Wall Street Journal, reading glasses, legs crossed, tired eyes. It doesn't take a rocket scientist, bud."

Dutch laughed. "So, what's the deal? You and your friends here for spring break?"

"*Spring break*? Like, do I look like a kid to you?"

My goodness no, Dutch wanted to say. "Difficult to tell these days."

"Now that's the truth. Some of these girls look old as me, and have the nerve to say they're fourteen and fifteen. I'm like, really? Fourteen? But it begs the point, doesn't it? About spring break? I mean, who plans a convention in Miami Beach during spring break? Like, who does that? Lawyers, that's who!"

"Ah, you're *lawyers*," Dutch said with a lift of surprise in his voice. He would have never guessed that she and her rowdy table companions were attorneys.

"Public Defenders to be more precise," Gina said. "We're at the East Coast Public Defenders convention. Every year one person from our office has to go. Since I'm the newbie on the block, that duty fell to me."

"A new attorney?"

"Brand new. Two months licensed. Most of us at that table are newbies, in fact, from up and down the coast. Except for the guys. Most of them are already successful attorneys in their own right, as their extra show of testosterone continually makes clear." Dutch smiled. "We're the brain brawl committee."

"The brain brawl committee?"

"Ain't it stupid?" she said with a smile so alluring that at that moment he wanted to kiss her. "But yeah, that's what they call it. We're supposed to come up with new and innovative ways to make our jobs less stressful. Like that's possible in big, urban areas where most of us work. These people crazy! But that's what they've tasked us with."

"And I take it you guys are loud and happy because you're making bounds of progress?"

"We're getting sloshed more like," Gina said and Dutch laughed. "But it's all bullshit in the end, anyway, right? A less stressful public defender's office? Come on. But those are the kind of assignments they love to give to geeks."

"Funny," Dutch said, smiling but meaning it, "I don't think geek when I look at you."

"That's because I'm not a geek. I'm just smart, or so they keep telling me. And keep selecting me for these ridiculous committees."

"So those folks at that table over there aren't your friends, but your brain brawl mates?"

"Exactly. And I hang out with them because I've never been in Miami a day in my life, wouldn't know where to begin to go, and the thought of sitting around alone in my hotel room, well, that wasn't very appealing either. So they asked, I said yes, and here I am. Apologizing on behalf of all of us."

Dutch liked her. He liked her instantly. "Apology accepted," he said.

9

Gina liked him, too. Found him attractive, too. A little older than she was used to, but still young enough. Well-built, but not flaunting it. "Well, Dutch," she said, about to rise, "I just wanted to let you know that we won't be here long, since they're talking about going to bed soon."

"Bed?" Dutch said before he realized it. "It's only ten."

"That's how geeks roll, what can I say?" He laughed. "But don't worry. We'll be out of your hair soon enough."

Dutch, however, didn't particularly want her out of his hair anytime soon. "What, are you the good will ambassador of the group?"

"That group? Get real! I just happen to look up and see you cringe over and over, so I decided to give you the heads up, that's all. And besides, getting away from that table breaks up the boredom."

"Boredom?" Dutch asked. "You're bored?"

"To tears. The only reason I came on this trip at all was because it's mandatory."

"But even so, Gina, this is spring break. Why are your brain brawl mates sitting up in here? Why aren't they out painting the town?"

"They're geeks," Gina said with laughter in her eyes. "They think they are painting the town."

Dutch laughed. "I see," he said, nodding his head, causing a thin strand of black hair to cascade down onto his forehead.

She kept looking at him. Yes, very attractive, she decided. And although she was five-seven herself, he was well over six feet tall, with a hard chest and sinewy arms, a flat stomach, and that strong, ultra-masculine face you often saw in commercials for cologne or shaving cream. A rich mane of black, silk-textured hair dropped down to his neck. Large, forest-green eyes underneath perfectly trimmed dark eyebrows that only enhanced the green in those eyes. A long, thin nose, full lips for a white guy, and a jaw line that was rugged but curved at just the right angle to make him gorgeous in a way that many women would walk past and then, realizing what beauty they'd just witnessed, turn and take another look.

It had been Gina's experience, however, that powerfully good looking men usually meant a powerfully good amount of trouble, something she wasn't about to get into right now, not when she was just beginning her career and just beginning to get over all of those other good looking men of her past.

"I'd better get back with the pack," she said, moving to leave for real this time. But Dutch touched her on her hand. She looked at his hand on hers, and then into his eyes. His tired-looking, but alluringly attractive forest-green eyes.

Dutch looked into her eyes, too. And hers were big, bright, sparkling oak-brown eyes. Her eyes popped, as his father used to say, with that glassy, almost dreamy gleam. "You didn't tell me your age," he said.

To his relief, she settled back into her seat. "Twenty-five," she said, "almost twenty-six."

"Ah, you're a baby," he said with a kidding smile.

"My baby days are long behind me," Gina said, smiling too. "Trust, okay?"

Dutch laughed, thoroughly enjoying himself. He, in fact, felt he had to keep asking questions, to keep the conversation going, to keep this interesting lady within his sight. "Why public defender?" he asked her. "Why not the private sector where your talents could fetch you top dollar?"

Gina thought about this. "It's not a question of money for me at this point," she said, "it's a question of where I'm needed, where I can be the most helpful."

"But you don't have time to do much help, do you, in a busy public defender's office? Except maybe move the cases along?"

"That's what the vets say, but I still plan to do some good. To make sure the poor get solid representation. Or what's the point, right? Because some of these sorry-behind PD's I'm seeing at this convention, and those I'm already seeing in my office back home, leaves a lot to be desired, I'm telling you."

He smiled at her passion and looked down from her adorable face, to her thin, graceful neck, to those breasts again. He could see his hands squeezing them, his mouth sucking them. He had come into this lounge in need of a woman. But he didn't just need this particular woman. He wanted her. And by night's end, he inwardly declared, he was going to do everything within his power to have her.

He didn't realize he was staring unblinkingly at her breasts until she had already stood up. And he was mortified. He could have kicked himself for being unable to control his ever-increasing lust.

"I'd better get back," she said this time without hesitation and before he could stand up or say anything that would encourage her to stay, she walked off.

Her very intelligent, very perceptive eyes had no doubt caught him assessing her, and probably didn't like it. She had to be used to it, a woman with all of her attributes. But she was also probably tired of it. Probably thought she had to get away from this old-ass pervert fast. Then he snorted, shook his head. Women used to fawn over him, now he was scaring them away. He was out of practice big time, he thought.

He tried to get back into his newspaper and forget about her, but he couldn't stop taking longer and longer glances at that table of attorneys, not just when they had bursts of laughter, but even when they were subdued. She was laughing with them, and hoisting up drinks, but he also noticed that she'd put the glass to her mouth but rarely took a sip, while all the others were slinging it down. There was a smart, sensible lady, he thought, as his eyes fixated on her face, trailed down to her breasts yet again, as his loins throbbed hard at just the thought of having sweet Gina in his bed.

Fat chance of that now, he also thought, as he drained down the last of his drink, tossed a fifty on the table, and stood to leave. He was too exhausted to care anymore, anyway. And besides, he had a ton of meetings tomorrow and needed to get some sleep.

As he turned to leave, however, he saw one of the attorneys, a very handsome young man, whisper something in Gina's ear. Without a second's hesitation, Gina took her glass and slung the liquid contents into the young man's face, causing him to immediately stand to his feet in shock at the sudden cold liquid chilling his body.

"Bitch!" the young attorney yelled and Dutch, his heart pounding, hurried to Gina's side just as that same young man moved to slap her. Dutch caught his arm just as he was about to inflict his retribution, and pulled his hand back.

"Not going to happen, pal," he said.

The young man turned to Dutch, surprised by his intervention, but saw a look in Dutch's eyes that made him back off of his aggression. And he slung away from Dutch's grasp.

Dutch looked at Gina. She looked more angry than flustered. "You okay?" he asked her.

"I'm fine," she said, staring at the young attorney, daring him to so much as think about hitting her.

"How about we get out of here?"

Gina continued to stare at her nemesis, as if deciding if the conflict was worth escalating. Then she exhaled, deciding not. "Sounds like a plan to me," she said, glancing once again at the attorney, and then she began to leave with Dutch.

"She'd better leave!" they could hear the young attorney boast, the anger still in his voice.

"You know how she is," added one of the females at the table. "They say she's crazy, anyway." And they all laughed.

Dutch and Gina headed through the colonnade, across the lobby, and up to one of the just-arrived elevators. They stepped on as an elderly couple stepped off.

"What's your room number?" Dutch asked her.

"Sixty-seven," she said as the doors closed. She hated confrontation, but she would give as good as she got any day of the week.

Dutch pressed the button to the sixth floor and leaned against the rail. She looked more vulnerable, and younger, than she had looked in the lounge.

"Are you sharing your room with any of your brain brawl friends?" he asked her.

She gave him a look that could melt steel.

He smiled. "Understood," he said, and then folded his arms. "So what was it that the kid said that caused you to drench him?"

Gina hesitated, didn't really feel like getting into it, and then sighed. It didn't matter. "He said he liked me," she said.

Dutch hesitated himself, expecting a punch line. When none came, he smiled. "And that caused the downpour? Because he said he liked you?"

"He said it for the hundredth time."

Dutch nodded. "I see." Then he stared at her longer, and as the elevator approached the sixth floor, decided it was now or never. "So if I were to say, for the first time that is, that I happen to like you, too, what would I be in for?"

Gina considered him. She'd already concluded that he was attracted to her, that didn't take a genius to figure out the way his eyes kept roaming all over her body. What she hadn't worked out, however, was if she wanted to bother. It would be a one-night stand, she would see to that, but she wasn't exactly the one night stand type. Hit and runs never appealed to her. There was something morally off-putting about them. But he was so adorable. And he did race to her defense, definite points there.

She decided to go with it. "What would you like to be in for?" she asked him.

Dutch's heart leaped with hopefulness. "Want the truth," he asked, staring deep into her eyes, unsure if she could handle it, "or bullshit?"

Gina almost smiled at his frankness, but maintained her cool. "I'll take the truth, if you don't mind," she replied, daring him to go there.

He went there. "I'd like to hold your beautiful body in my arms, to be deep inside of you, to fuck you so long and so hard that I make you feel unlike any other man before me ever had."

Gina expected some truth, and some predictable bravado thrown in, but nothing on this order. Her entire face flushed hot. But she found she liked his bluntness. "Well," she said, staring into his eyes. Then she thought about it further, and then exhaled as if she'd reached a conclusion. "That'll certainly beat a brain brawl any day of the week," she said, and Dutch, overjoyed, laughed.

The elevator lurched to a stop and prepared to open at the sixth floor, and she moved to unload. But Dutch took her by the hand. "Certain you want to do this?" he asked her.

"Certain, no," she said thoughtfully, as the elevator binged and the doors began to open, "but I want to do it."

He pulled her toward him. "Then stay on," he said. "We'll go to my room." *In case your attorney friends decide to interrupt us in yours*, he wanted to add.

A family piled onto the elevator and the doors closed again. Dutch turned Gina's body so that she would face him when he noticed the father of the family taking peeps at her large breasts.

Gina smiled, understanding why Dutch did it. "Protective, are we?" she asked in jest.

"With what's mine," Dutch said with all seriousness, "oh, yeah."

TWO

The door closed behind them as they entered his hotel room, and the sound of silence made them realize that they were now on the road of no return. Because as quickly as the door slammed shut, a sexual energy entered like a searing wildfire in the once drab room. A room, Gina noted, that was just like hers, which surprised her. She expected a man of his obvious stature to have a suite, or at least something more substantial. Unless spring break reservationists had already taken the best rooms, and he had to get what was left. Then she realized what she was doing, that she was finding something to distract, which meant she was far more nervous than she was letting on.

"What would you like to drink?" Dutch asked her.

"Whatever you're drinking suits me."

"Smart lady," he said with a smile and headed for the wet bar.

Gina walked around the small room, watching him as he poured drinks. He'd already made perfectly clear what he wanted to do to her, and she'd assented. She loved truth. She loved bluntness. That was why she didn't beat around the bush, playing any core games, and sat on the bed. They weren't friends. They weren't even lovers. They were just two people who wanted to get laid, would get laid, and, as far as she was concerned, that would be the end of it.

He walked over to the bed and handed her a glass of wine, pleased by her lack of insecurity.

"Thanks," she said as she crossed her legs and leaned back on the palm of her hand.

But yet, Dutch thought, as he couldn't take his eyes off of her, she had an innocence about her, a sweetness even. Big, bright eyes, smooth, unblemished skin, a naturalness to her that was refreshing to him. "How old are you, Gina?" he asked her as he sipped his drink.

"Why do you keep asking me that?" Gina wanted to know. "Twenty-five, remember? I'm legal. How old are you?"

"Don't ask," he said with a smile, sat his glass on the nightstand, and began removing his suit coat and unbuttoning his shirt. Once his shirt was unbuttoned, revealing a muscular chest and a ribbed-line, flat stomach, he moved up to Gina, standing like a towering figure of strength in front of her.

"Do you want to play cute games," he asked her, "laugh coquettishly at stale jokes, delay the inevitable, or get on with it?"

Gina smiled. She liked his style. "Get on with it, please," she said.

He removed her glass and sat it on the nightstand also, and then, without hesitation, leaned down, his hands resting on either side of her, and kissed her ever so gently on her lips.

There was a gentleness to his kiss, a kind of warm, sweet easiness. She closed her eyes, drinking in his taste, enjoying him.

As his kissing slowed, he looked into her eyes. Made sure she was still with him. Then he did what he had been itching to do since he first laid eyes on her, and took the straps of her dress and pulled them down, past her breasts, to her waist.

When he pulled her dress down, her plump, fully erect breasts popped out like two brown melons, juicy and ripe. Dutch stood tall and stared at Gina, as he slowly, expertly caressed her breasts, his big hands rubbing and then squeezing , soothing and then caressing. Gina stared back at Dutch, her big, brown eyes filled with a kind of wonderment that would make a man feel almost heroic.

But Gina couldn't help it. He was backing up his big talk. He knew how to finesse it, just the way she loved it. She was accustomed to men seeing her bare breasts and, realizing they were natural issue, no enhancements whatsoever, would go nuts and began squeezing too hard or sucking too long and making her feel like some kind of rubber toy, rather than a woman.

Dutch, however, didn't have that problem. He loved the way she felt in his hands, and moving along quickly was not an option. He looked from those magnetic eyes of hers, to those lips again, and he found himself licking his. And kissing her passionately on those lips as he continued to caress her breasts.

He got on his knees as his lips moved down to her breasts, and he began to suck, to tease, and ultimately to put her nipples, one by one, and then both of them, into his mouth. Gina loved the feeling of his mouth on her breasts, at the intensity when he sucked her nipples.

He studied her face as he began fondling her breasts again, his look as purposeful as a doctor looking on at his anesthetized patient.

Gina was aware of his stare, but more aware of how he was making her feel. She looked up at him as he fondled her, and his breath caught. Something about her turned him on so completely. But he kept seeing innocence when he looked into her eyes.

"Sure you can handle me?" he asked her.

Gina smiled. He was certainly sure of himself. "I can handle it," she said.

Dutch kept staring anyway, at that little face. She had a look about her, a sense and style about her, that seemed to personify something that mere beauty just didn't capture. She was strong, and her own person, and determined, it was all in her bright brown eyes. But a sweetness was in those eyes too, a kind of trusting that seemed to belie her outward expressions of strength. That was why he stared. That was why he kept wanting to make sure she could handle this.

His eyes trailed down, from her expressive eyes, to her velvety brown skin, to her full, adorable lips. His eyes stayed on her lips. Especially when she smiled, revealing those beautiful white teeth that highlighted stunningly her dark skin. He put his lips on hers, felt the instant heat, and kissed her once again.

The kiss was a long, circular kiss this time, where he was tasting her and she was tasting him and they both decided that they were enjoying the meal. Gina usually hated, absolutely abhorred when a guy put his mouth on hers. But not this time. She was amazed at how much she enjoyed it. This man knew what he was doing.

Dutch had expected her to taste sweet, she had that kind of mouth, but he never dreamed she'd be this delectable. He stood up, took her by the shoulders and stood her up from the bed, and got a taste of her in full. They embraced as his tongue explored hers in a tease of pent-up sexual tension that had been bubbling within him for far too long. And she was the perfect woman to release on. Oh, how wonderful she tasted to him! He closed his eyes and could have continued kissing her for hours, his mouth moving around and around over hers. And her curvaceous, pliable body in his arms made him begin to understand why that young man so wanted her to like him.

When they stopped kissing and Dutch looked at her, he didn't see any superwoman sex maven, but a lost kid, searching for love in all the wrong places, surprised that just a kiss could feel this good. And it disturbed him. Was she really ready for this?

Although Gina didn't feel like the lost kid he may have been making her out to be, she was, however, surprised. She'd had her share of boyfriends in her past, and she thought she'd seen and felt all there was to this sex thing. But in the hands of this man, she'd felt the kind of longing for affection she never dreamed was possible to feel. Sex for her had always been a tiresome chore, something she simply had to endure to get where she needed to go, which was the affection part, which usually didn't show up in the end anyway. But this man was affection personified. Especially when he placed his hand on her chin, and gently lifted her face up to his.

"Sure you want to go through with this?" he asked her. He would die where he stood if she wasn't sure, his manhood was throbbing just that aggressively, but by that bewildered look in her eyes, he had to ask it.

Gina stared into his own expressive eyes. Was this guy for real, or what, she wondered? What man would care if she wanted to go through with anything? They'd have her on that bed fucking her brains out regardless of what she wanted. She agreed to do it and they wouldn't care what she felt after that agreement.

But this guy was different. He seemed so genuine. His kind, soft eyes seemed so concerned. Of course, he could be a master player who was so good at the game that Gina didn't even know she was being played. But somehow, looking into his eyes, she doubted that.

And the thought of not going through with this, with this man, was a joke to her. No way was she turning back now. "Yes, I'm sure," she said heartfelt and Dutch smiled. And an enchanting smile it was, Gina thought, as she found herself staring at his perfect teeth. Did this man have any flaws, she wondered? But of course he did. And big time flaws at that. Why else, she reasoned, would a great looking, apparently successful dude like him need to spend his evening with some just beginning her career kid like her?

Dutch, however, couldn't think of anyone else he would rather be with. He found everything about her pleasing. He couldn't say why. He couldn't point to anything about her that would seal the deal and make him label her the most gorgeous maven he'd ever had.

But there was something about her that touched him on a different level. He saw more than mere gorgeousness when he looked at her. And as he continued to remove her dress, and her panties completely, as his loins began to pulsate at the thought of fucking her, he *felt* her looks more than he saw them. As if her true attractiveness was beyond the surface, and was alive with vitality and energy, the kind of attractiveness that would make the most beautiful of beauty queens look plain, drab, and so ordinary that, compared to her, they wouldn't look beautiful at all.

Dutch removed his clothes just as quickly as he had undressed her, rendering them both completely naked.

Gina had always made it her business to never stare at a her sex partner's body, or at least not blatantly stare, but she couldn't help herself this time. She stared unblinkingly at Dutch's strapping frame, from his muscular chest, to his flat, rib-lined stomach, to his big, fat manhood that dangled before her like a powerful, jewel ready to be possessed. She'd never seen one quite this big, which wasn't a complete stretch since she hadn't seen *that* many. But the sight of it, and the possibility of what that thick rod could do to her, caused her to intake air in a loud, sensual sigh.

Dutch smiled when he heard her reaction to how well he was hung. He was accustomed to such a reaction from females, but he was exceptionally pleased to see it in this woman before him. To him it only confirmed his suspicion. She wasn't anywhere near as experienced as her natural self-assuredness made her out to be.

Gina tried to pivot from the point of admiration to actively participating in this affair, but after she reached out and touched his rod, and began caressing its long, thick form, something in him, some level of control, began to break. He lifted her into his arms and laid her onto the bed, kissing her breasts, her stomach, spreading her legs, her sweet, womanly scent intoxicating him. But he didn't want to rush it. He moved up and began kissing her again. But this time it was with more hunger, his lips bearing down on hers hard.

She could feel his ever-expanding penis press against her womanhood, as he couldn't seem able to stop kissing her. Not that she wanted him to stop, because she didn't. But she was amazed at his ability to hold out.

By the way he kissed her, it was surprising that they'd only just met, as her body began to match his in a passion that would have been shared more by long-time couples than one-night-stands. This wasn't sex. She knew sex. This was love making, a kind of sweet, wonderful, enchanting sensuality she'd never experienced before.

He moved down the length of her magnificent body, kissing and caressing as he moved. When he reached her thighs, he again parted her legs and began to explore her womanhood with his fingers, one stroke at a time, one finger at a time, and then both fingers, sliding in and out of her, making her ready, making her wet.

He knew he didn't know her like this, but he couldn't help it. He kissed her womanhood, and he couldn't stop kissing and licking and eating it. He wanted her so badly that he looked up at her, moved back up the length of her, and almost entered her raw. He wanted to enter her raw.

But Gina was not that far gone, and she stopped him.   He may have been able to make her feel unlike anybody else had ever before, but he was still a man. He put on a condom.

Dutch entered her slowly, his penis expanding the further in he moved. He looked at her as he explored her, as his penis moved in circular motions, touching her in such a way that she could feel the friction to every inch deep inside of her. And this woman who was supposed to be so tough, had tears in her eyes as he fucked her. He laid down on top of her, and pulled her into his arms. He'd never felt this kind of connection before, not this kind, and he didn't want it to end.

That was why he kept it slow and steady, gyrating his big, naked body in a rhythm that he didn't even realize he knew. Now he seemed like the master of its beat, moving in and out of her, inundating her with just the right slow drag that they both felt nearly drunk with sensuality.

For the longest time they gyrated together, like a slow drag they didn't want to end, especially as the music was reaching it crescendo.

And when he began to release, he could feel it pour out of him and into her, and he began to pump harder, and faster as it poured, making sloshing sounds as it poured, as it slid down the sides of her thighs in a warm, sticky, silkiness. And when the feeling reached its apex and then began to descend, they both lifted up too, in a spasm of tight, tense, beautifully explosive feelings, and then crashed back down. They felt together. They felt intoxicated. They felt, each in their own way, breathtakingly alive.

And when it was over, and Dutch rolled off of her, he pulled her into his arms. Neither one of them knew what to say. This was crazy. This was supposed to be a hit and run, a roll in the hay, wasn't that what this night was supposed to be about?

They didn't know what to feel, or think, or say, so they didn't feel, think, or say anything. They just lay there, in each other's arms, until the quietness overtook them, and they fell asleep.

He woke up later that night to find her gone. No goodbye, no note, gone. And he almost panicked. He knew she was on the sixth floor, although he didn't know her room number nor her last name come to that, but he got out of bed and slipped in his pants anyway, ready to go find her room even if he had to knock on every door.

But his secondary cell phone rang. Only three people in this world had that particular number. His mother, his father, and his best friend and family attorney, Max Brennan.

It was Max. "Get to Nantucket, Dutch," he said before Dutch could say hello. The family compound was on Nantucket Island.

"What's happened?" Dutch asked.

"It's your father. It's Pop's." There was a hesitation. Then an enormous sigh. "He's dead, my friend," Max said, a cry in his voice. "Pop's dead."

Dutch's father had been in and out of hospitals a lot over the last few years, his heart not working quite right was the problem. And his death should not have come as a shock to anyone.

But it was a shock to Dutch. It shook him to his core. And the idea of looking for anyone, of knocking on anybody's hotel room door to begin some hot and heavy romance with what faced him now, was thoroughly out of the question.

THREE

TEN YEARS LATER

The ceremony was to take place in the East Room of the White House, and Regina Lansing, along with her business partner and best friend, Loretta "LaLa" King, were among the invited guests. Not because she was some hot shot DC lobbyist or otherwise well-connected politico, but because her Newark, New Jersey organization, the Block by Block Raiders, was among those non-profit groups selected from across the country to receive the prestigious Presidential Mountain Movers award. And the president himself would be the presenter.

"Ladies and gentlemen," the announcer said in a deep, roaring voice, "the President of the United States!"

Hail to the Chief music began to blare throughout the room and everybody stood to their feet. Gina was so nervous she could hear her heart pounding as she stood in anticipation of the president's arrival. Would he remember her? Or was that night as forgettable for him as it was memorable for her?

Her bet was that he simply didn't remember her. After all, it was a decade ago and he seemed to her to be a well-experienced hand at one-night stands. But even if he did remember, and to avoid any questions they decided to rescind the award, that wouldn't stop her goal. She wasn't here just to collect some award. She was mainly here to shine a light on the government's disastrous budget cuts that were decimating programs like hers. And when it was her time to get on that stage and give her acceptance speech on behalf of Block by Block Raiders, or BBR as they called it, she was going to make her feelings clear. If the president didn't veto Congress's upcoming budget requests, BBR and many organizations like it would have to close its doors.

And even when the president entered, walking his fine self onto the stage with that elegant, controlled stride he was famous for, and the entire room seemed to get a jolt of giddy excitement just by his presence alone, she was still determined to stand her ground.

She remembered him. It was years ago, but she remembered it as if it was last night. She remembered his big body on top of hers, gyrating her in such an expert way that she left that hotel suite in a daze. And his rod, she still had dreams about that thick rod inside of her, caressing and then pounding her, all stiff and hard.

She found out that he was her one-night-stand early in his political career, when he was first thrust onto the national stage some eight years ago as the newly elected senator from the great state of Massachusetts. He was known back then as the CEO Senator, a man with plenty of business expertise but no previous political experience. It was perfect timing back then since the electorate was tired of career politicians, and he quickly made his mark as a moderate, new kind of democrat.

She'd never met him personally early in his term, nor paid him much attention whenever she was lobbying Congress, until she saw him one night on CSPAN, giving an impassioned speech about the clean air act. His hair style was different, and he'd aged, but she suddenly realized that the handsome and bachelor Senator Walter Harber was the same man she had gotten to know quite intimately one sultry night in Miami Beach.

And when he decided to run for president and won three years ago, she was astounded. She wanted to tell somebody about it, she was that excited, but she didn't tell a soul. How would bragging about the fact that the then future President of the United States once had his way with her, be a positive for her?

Dutch Harber entered the East Room of the White House feeling as if it was déjà vu. This was his third ceremony of the morning. The first two, both also commemorating unique organizations, were brief and unremarkable. And when he welcomed the cheering room to the White House, and took a seat on the makeshift stage with the other dignitaries, he expected more of the same.

He would stand and present the award to each representative who came on stage, and then he'd sit back down while they gave their prepared remarks. His attention, however, would drift from the stage to the audience. Because he'd heard it all before. But after more than a few predictable acceptance speeches, his eyes drifted and stayed on one audience member in particular.

She sat on the front row, and during the entire ceremony she remained almost stoic, even bored. She never clapped. She never smiled. She never showed anything but seeming disinterest in the ceremony itself. But Dutch Harber couldn't take his eyes off of her.

He'd noticed her from the moment he arrived in the East Room, the audience rising and *Hail to the Chief* blaring in his ears. She was the youngest of the organization representatives, he'd noticed. Much younger. In Dutch's trained eyes, no more than thirty-five if she was a day.

He'd also noticed that she was the only female in the room who chose to wear pants rather than the conservative, button-down skirt and blazer that were standard issue around DC. She, in fact, wore a striking eggshell-white pantsuit that contrasted beautifully against her dark brown skin, with a royal purple blouse that crisscrossed at her ample breasts and revealed what he considered to be a tasteful amount of cleavage. Her heels were four-inches high, a magnificent golden-yellow, with a matching gold scarf wrapped neatly at her throat in an elegant overlay that made her look almost regal. His loins were throbbing just looking at her.

And her face. That was, for Dutch, the most intriguing feature of all. She wasn't someone he would pick out of a crowd and declare the most gorgeous woman he'd ever seen. He doubt if he could even declare her the most gorgeous woman in the room right at that moment.

But she was attractive in a way that beggared description. Her features were all African, especially her full lips and big, almond eyes with orbs as white as snow against pupils that were so deep brown that they seemed, at a distance, as black as coal. Her eyelashes swung out and curved over so enticingly that they gave one of her eyes, her right eye, a sexy droopiness. Her hair was styled in long, thin braids that swept down her back and looked simply divine to Dutch on her perfectly-formed, small head.

She had a strong look, a look that bespoke intelligence and confidence rather than coquettishness and frailty. And she had a quiet, sweet sensuality that hovered over her like an aphrodisiac. She, unlike anybody else he'd met in a long time, got his attention.

To Gina Lansing, however, she had no clue she was getting his attention, but she was certain she was about to get his wrath when it was her turn to take the stage. He was super calm, she thought, as she couldn't help but take peeps at the man. He sat elegantly on that stage in his expensive blue suit and tie, his long legs crossed, his intense, intelligent forest-green eyes focused away from the stage as each representative of each winning organization gave their prepared remarks.

She had to admit he was an impressive figure to behold, even better looking than she remembered him ten years ago. His jet-black, silky straight hair was now worn slicked back into a Wall Street, severe, conservative cut, and his sharp-tailored suit made him look as if he knew he was King of the mountain, but also knew how to ride that throne. On any other day, under any other circumstances, he would probably be an interesting person to get to know. But she didn't come here to get to know the President of the United States. She came here to shame him into action.

"Sure you still wanna do this?" LaLa leaned over and whispered in her ear. She was seated beside Gina and was everything Gina was not: short, heavyset, and so down-to-earth that she could almost seem rude.

"I've got to do it," Gina whispered back. "If he isn't prepared to veto that appropriations bill, our doors will have to close, no ands, ifs, or buts about it."

"You don't have to tell me that," LaLa said, "I know all that. But damn, girl," LaLa added, looking Dutch up and down, "that white man fine."

If you only knew how fine, Gina was almost tempted to say. "Don't be disrespectful," she said instead. "He's the president, after all."

"A president who can't take his eyes off of you."

Gina's heart beat a little faster. She had noticed it, too. But it didn't seem like a look of recognition or, as LaLa would suggest, attraction. It just seemed like he was bored by the ceremony and needed somebody to observe.

Besides, LaLa was always convinced every man wanted Gina. "That man is not thinking about me, okay?" she said to put an end to any wild speculations LaLa was known for.

"Uh-hun, if you say so," LaLa said, unconvinced. Then she leaned over to Gina again. "And what you mean 'don't be disrespectful?' You're the one planning to shame the man into action. That ain't disrespectful?"

"Of course not," Gina whispered back as if it was the most obvious thing in the world. *I pray not*, she inwardly said.

"And now," said the Master-of-Ceremony, a tall, wiry man, "the next success story is the Newark, New Jersey-based Block by Block Raiders. This organization began as the dream of a young one-time public defender who stayed in her hometown and sought to change the lives of troubled youth in her blighted urban neighborhood. Since its' inception five years ago, young gang members have quit the gang life and are now contributing members of society. The same for former prostitutes and drug addicts. Many of the residents of her community credit BBR with changing the entire trajectory of the young people's lives. That, in and of itself ladies and gentlemen, is an achievement. Let's therefore welcome Miss Regina Lansing to the stage to accept the award on behalf of Block by Block Raiders. Miss Lansing, ladies and gentlemen."

As they had done for the other organization reps, Dutch and all of the onstage dignitaries stood and applauded as Gina made her way onto the stage.

Oh, how lovely, Dutch thought as she walked onto the stage, her movements an education in grace and dignity. And when he gave her the framed award certificate, and reached out and shook her hand, her smile seemed so warm, so oddly familiar, that it took him aback. And he suddenly felt as if he knew her.

Gina felt a bolt of electricity when his hand touched hers, when she remembered what those hands once did to her. And when she looked into his kind, glassy, forest-green eyes, she found herself smiling. Smiling? She was about to rip him wide open, tear this mutha up with some truth, and she was smiling? She got serious again, accepted the award from him, and stood at the podium to give what they all undoubtedly assumed would be her prepared, staid remarks.

When everyone was seated and silence came into the room like a sudden cloud, she thanked the president and all of those assembled, exhaled in nervous exasperation, and then told it like the reality of BBR's situation decided that she had to.

"This award," she said as she stood behind the podium and stared at the certificate in her hand, the president, along with other dignitaries, seated not ten feet from her, "is without question the highest honor our small, truly grassroots organization will ever

receive. Without question. And we thank-you
for it. But, Mr. President," she said this as she
turned sideways to look directly at Dutch Harber,
"this award isn't worth the paper it's printed
on."

There was an audible gasp from the audience,
an audience that included a pool reporter and
cameraman with a live feed going to the 24-hour
cable news channels. It was obvious the
reporter had expected Gina's speech to be more
of the same because he was on his Blackberry
more than he was watching. Until she said her
not worth the paper it's printed on line. He
looked up then.

Dutch stared at her as she spoke, at the way
her eyes showed strength, but also a kind of sad
familiar yearning he could not place. But she
kept on.

"You've been in office for almost three years
now, sir, and you're a Democrat. But your
policies have been as destructive to
organizations like mine as any Republican
president has ever been. You say you're a
champion of at-risk youth in America, and many
of my colleagues have stood on this stage and

praised you for your work in that area. But talking is cheap where I come from, sir, and your actions speak a different reality than your words."

Gina hesitated, as her nerves were trying to get the best of her, as his eyes seemed so intensely glued to hers. But she continued. "Your administration has cut funding for organizations like mine two years in a row, and those cuts, sir, have been devastating. I know we have a serious budget deficit, I know everybody has got to take a hit, but you're trying to balance the budget on the backs of the very people who can least afford to take that big a hit."

She exhaled again, had to relax her nerves again. "I used to admire you, sir. When you got elected I sighed relief. Finally, I thought, we had a fighter in the White House, a fighter for the poor and disenfranchised. But you have been a huge disappointment, sir. A huge disappointment."

Dutch's heart sank at the thought of her being disappointed in him, but he was a master politician and continued to sit there, hands in lap, legs crossed, as if her entire diatribe had nothing to do with him.

Gina kept on. "If you truly want to be the champion of at-risk youth you claim to be, then you'd put your foot down and stop compromising with those Republicans who seek to punish people simply because they never had the same advantages others had. If all you see is success around you, then you'd be successful too. But if all you see is failure around you, as the young people I work with are bombarded with day in and day out, then guess which outcome you're more likely to have?"

She looked at the award again, an award, if she wasn't fighting for her organization's life, she'd be proud to accept. "This award is nice, and it'll make leaders of organizations like mine very happy and pleased, but it doesn't feel right. It feels like a sell-out, to be honest with you. It feels like I'm supposed to pretend that my government is actually on my side, ready and willing to help our at-risk youth, when nothing could be further from the truth. Thanks, Mr. President," she said lastly, "but no thanks."

And then she walked off of the stage, leaving the award on the podium. The same audience that had applauded all of the previous speakers at the end of their speeches, sat mute at the end of hers.

The sudden tension in the room was palpable, with all angst directed, not at President Harber, but at Gina herself. Even LaLa was amazed. She expected a tough speech, but nothing *that* blunt. She leaned over to her colleague as soon as she took her seat. "That man is not pleased," she said of the president.

But Gina merely sat up tall and kept looking forward. She didn't come to please the president. She came to make a point. A point, she felt, given the sudden silence in the room, she absolutely felt she made.

The Master of Ceremony took to the podium again and didn't miss a beat. "Our next winning organization," he said as he continued the program. This was DC, after all, inside the Beltway, and they knew how to pretend everything was peaches and cream when it was more like sour cream. Dutch pretended too, as he redirected his attention to the Master of Ceremony and the next organization rep.

But his peace was disturbed. She was *disappointed* in me, he kept saying to himself. And her words, her carefully crafted, blunt words, felt like a knife jab to his heart.

Why it bothered him in such a personal way when he was well accustomed to political attacks by the biggest bomb throwers in the business, many of whom were elected members of Congress, he'd never know. But it bothered him fiercely.

After the ceremony was over and the President and other dignitaries had already left the room, the crowd began to file out also. LaLa, who had her hand on Gina's shoulder as if she had to shepherd her out, joked about how the other organization representatives were avoiding Gina like the plague. "They think your truthfulness is contagious," she said with a smile.

"Ain't it something," Gina replied. "You'd think I was up there lying on the man."

"Honey, I know. But who cares about these holier-than-Thou stuff shirts? Their organizations are hurting because of these budget cuts just like ours, and they're probably glad you spoke up, but nobody will admit it publicly. Besides, they probably think people like us don't deserve any presidential award anyway, have no right being anywhere near this White House, and your outburst, they feel, just proved their point. Well I say bump'em."

Gina smiled at LaLa's choice of words.

"Miss Lansing," a male's voice said from behind and Gina and LaLa both turned to the sound. He was a blonde-haired, blue-eyed young man, in a rumpled suit and bowtie.

"Yes?" Gina said.

"Hi, I'm Christian Bale. I know," he said kind of geeky-like. "But no, I'm not the actor. I'm the president's assistant. He wishes, that is, the president wishes to see you, ma'am."

Gina's heart dropped. "To see me?"

"Yes, ma'am."

"Why would he want to see me?"

"Why?" Christian said as if he could not believe her lack of insight. "Well, let me see. It may have something to do with the fact that you just told him off on national TV. I don't know, he doesn't share his innermost thoughts with me, but I'm just saying."

He reminded Gina of LaLa: a jokey, almost flippant quality about him. She, in fact, looked at LaLa.

"What you looking at me for?" LaLa said. "The man is the President of the United States. It ain't like you got a choice." Then she exhaled, and her look turned serious, more somber. "I'll meet you back at the hotel, girl," she said. "And, Gina," she added as she began to leave, "don't get blinded by the lights. What you said today needed to be said, whether these other organizations, or the president himself, gives you credit or not. You told the truth."

Gina nodded and stiffened her resolve. "Okay, Christian," she said with more gusto, "take me to your leader."

Christian smiled. What a piece of work, he thought. "This way, ma'am," he said.

FOUR

Christian's "leader" was her leader too, in fact the leader of the free world, and to her surprise she wasn't taken to some side office on the West Wing, or even to the Oval office, but to what Christian said was the West sitting room of the second-floor residence. It was a less formal room in an almost living room style, with a big, lunette window that overlooked well-known landmarks like the Old Executive Office Building, a room with a yellow sofa, flanking arch-top chairs in pastel colors, sweeping gold curtains with yellow and blue trim.

Gina took a seat on the yellow sofa and Christian sat with her. Although he seemed willing to talk, she mainly kept her own counsel. It wasn't every day that a girl like her got to have an audience with the president. The president! And it was exciting her in a way she didn't think that it would.

But LaLa was right. She wasn't going to be blinded by the lights. She'd just, in Christian's words, "told off" that same President and he was probably royally pissed. And the fact that they'd met before under circumstances neither could want public, made clear that this meeting wasn't going to be a congratulatory one.

He arrived nearly an hour after she and Christian had been seated. And as soon as he arrived, both she and Christian stood up.

"Sit down, sit down," Dutch said, moving fast across the room toward the large wet bar. "Have a drink, Miss Lansing? Did you offer her a drink, Chris?"

Christian's already pale face turned ghostly. "Ah, no, sir, I'm sorry, sir, I didn't think--"

"What would you care to drink, Miss Lansing?" Dutch asked, pouring himself a drink.

"Nothing for me, thanks," Gina said.

"Nothing? Nothing at all?"

Gina started to say water, just to sound non-combative, but she didn't want water. Or anything else. "No, nothing," she said. Then awkwardly added: "Sir."

This felt almost surreal to her, sitting in the White House residence, being offered a drink by Dutch Harber. She was almost waiting for Ashton Kutcher to jump out of a closet and announce that she'd been punk'd.

Dutch grabbed his drink and headed for the sofa where Gina was seated. Although Gina had sat back down when Dutch urged them to, Christian remained standing. Gina was about to stand again, but Dutch motioned her back down. And then he gave Christian a look that could chill the sun. Gina wasn't certain what it meant, but Christian was. He promptly bowed nervously and hurried out of the room. How a nervous man like him got a job as the aide to a take-no-prisoners politician like Dutch Harber, was beyond Gina.

"He worked his butt off for me during my campaign," Dutch answered her unasked question. "He's a very discreet young man. Very discreet. I trust him with my life." He said this as he took a seat, not in the chair flanking the sofa, but next to her on the comfortable, yellow sofa.

And the mere thought of it, that she was sitting next to the most powerful man in the world, caused her entire body to suddenly feel constricted. She swallowed hard and then looked at him. She kept trying not to think about that night in Miami Beach, but she kept failing. Her eyes roamed down, from his magnificent face with that strong jaw she remembered so well, to his muscle-tight chest.

"So," Dutch said, as he crossed his leg, unbuttoned his suit coat, and turned his body toward her, "you're the young lady who ate my lunch this afternoon."

Gina smiled at the way he had put it. "Christian said I told you off."

"That too," Dutch said with a smile of his own, a smile that didn't quite reach his eyes. Mainly because he was too busy thinking about her, about how she looked even lovelier when she smiled. And her sizeable breasts, the way they heaved up whenever she began to speak, made his loins began to pulsate. "I know you're Miss Lansing, but I can't recall your first name."

"Regina. Although all of my friends call me
Gina." Gina said this and looked at him, to see if
her nickname spurred him to remember.

It didn't. "Gina it is," he said, and extended
his hand. "I'm Walt Harber, Gina, although all of
my friends call me Dutch."

Gina shook his hand. "I know. Your nickname
is the most famous nickname in the world. But
why, is what I've always wanted to know."

"Why is it so famous?" he asked, unwilling to
let go of her hand.

"Why are you called Dutch to begin
with. How did that come about? Are you of
Dutch ancestry or something?"

Dutch laughed. "No, nothing like that. You
ever hear the phrase 'going Dutch?'"

"You mean where you go out on a date and
each person pays for her own food?" Gina had
to make extra effort to remove her hand from
his tight hold.

"Correct," Dutch said, disappointed that she
had released his grasp. "When I was a very
young man in high school and would take young
ladies out on dates, I was a strict adherent to
that rule. One young lady who didn't much like

the rule, started calling me Dutch Harber, the guy who makes the ladies pay. From that day to this I've been Dutch Harber. But that's a label for you. It tends to stick."

Gina agreed. "You don't seem like the type who would make a lady pay her own way."

"Oh, but I am. Very much so. I like my women strong and independent. Able to handle their business." He looked down at Gina's breasts, and then back up into her eyes, with a hooded, lustful look he wasn't attempting to hide. "A woman like you, Regina."

Gina didn't quite know how to take that comment. Nor that look. Although she presented as this tower of strength, she didn't see herself that way at all. The idea of a man taking care of her, and doing things for her, was romantic in her eyes, something she would probably enjoy. But since she'd never had the chance to find out if she'd enjoy it or not, she never wasted much time thinking about it. "I don't know if I'm all that strong," she said, attempting to laugh it off.

"You may not know it, but I do."

"You?" Gina asked, wondering if he remembered Miami after all.

"Yes, me."

"But you don't know jack about me."

Dutch smiled. "I know that any female willing to stand before the President of the United States and call him everything but a child of God, has got to be strong."

Gina laughed. He loved the way her narrow shoulders shook when she did. "I like that about you," he added, unable to share in her laughter.

Gina felt the heat of his stare all over her body. He seemed determined to make it clear to her that he was interested. Which would be remarkable in and of itself. This man was the president, for crying out loud! But she was no fool, either. He was the very eligible bachelor President, a man who had lost his fiancée a decade ago in a plane crash and had, after mourning her death, decided to play the field liberally.

According to press reports she remembered reading during the campaign, he was known in some circles as *Wham Bam Harber*, the hit and run specialist. The man who often played the field.

And now this same man was showing interest in her? But why? Did he remember her and, more importantly, did he see her as an easy lay? Did he figure he could have some quickie, some booty call session with a powerless female like her, then dump her quietly because nobody but her powerless self would care? She decided to test the waters, to see if she was right.

"Is this why you asked to see me? Because you think I'm tough?"

"I didn't say you were tough," Dutch corrected her. "You aren't tough. But you're strong. And yes, that's part of it."

"What's the other part?" Gina asked, unsure what he meant. "The fact that you agree with me and will veto that budge bill?"

"I can't commit to that at this point."

"But why, sir? I don't think you understand how all of these rounds and rounds of budget cuts are affecting programs like mine. In this bad economy, all of our private donations have completely dried up. Not that they were outstanding to begin with. I mean, who wants to give money to an organization that helps gang bangers and prostitutes get their acts together? Who wants justice for those former criminals, right?"

It was the word justice that stopped Dutch cold. And he remembered. He remembered the MC at the awards ceremony mentioning that she used to be a public defender. And her passion for the poor and misbegotten. And her nickname is Gina. And she has those striking eyes and curvaceous figure and . . . But It *couldn't be*, he thought.

Unaware that his look had changed dramatically toward her, Gina kept talking. "So private donations have never been our driving force," she continued. "It was government grants that kept our doors open. But if Congress keeps cutting that funding, our revenue stream will dry up so completely that we won't have any choice but to shut down. And Block by Block Raiders is a very successful organization, we don't have to pad our numbers the way a lot of these other non-profits do. We're for real, sir."

Dutch was certain now. It was her. It was that wonderful young lady in Miami Beach all those years ago. The one that had rocked his world for that one night. The night of his father's death. He had been so traumatized by succeeding events, so swept up by the enormous burden he immediately had to bear as the heir to his father's fortune, that he tried his level best not to entertain memories of that wonderful night. He became so successful at compartmentalizing his life before and after his father's death, so spot-on with his singular focus, that, over time, his memories of that night began to fade to such an extent that they became no memories at all.

Until now.

When Gina realized she was getting no response from the president, she looked at him. And that lustful look she had seen earlier was now replaced with a look of alarm. "What is it?" she asked him. "What's the matter?"

Dutch didn't know how to play this. Had she forgotten about Miami? About that night?

"You're the founder of Block by Block Raiders?" he asked her.

Gina was spooked now. He recognized her, she could tell it by that unsettled, stormy look in his eyes. "Yes, sir," she said cautiously. What, she wondered, would he do with his knowledge?

"You call it BBR?"

"That's right."

"It helps former gang members and, and prostitutes, with their legal issues, among other things, right?"

"Right."

"Because you're an attorney. The MC mentioned you were a former public defender."

Ah, there it was, she thought. It was out there now. "That's right," she said.

Dutch nodded, sipped from his wine. Found himself looking down at her breasts, remembering how he once sucked them. He began to rub his forehead. "From Newark?"

Gina smiled. "Yes." He definitely remembered.

Dutch was stunned he hadn't put it together sooner. Although the days following their encounter were pretty much a blur as funeral arrangements and business meetings took a front seat to any one-night-stand, her image would still cross his mind. He couldn't count how many times, early on, he considered tracking her down, to find her, to keep her as his.

But life kept getting in the way and the responsibilities kept compounding, making it impossible for him to track anybody anywhere. And by the time he was urged to go into politics, a lifelong dream of his father's, remembering one night stands in beach hotels was about as productive for the reality of his life as a hole in the head.

"You remember that night, don't you, Gina?" he asked her pointblank.

Gina nodded. "Yes, sir."

He let out a grim sigh. Began rubbing his forehead again. "And you've shared that information with?"

Gina frowned. "Nobody. Why would I share something like that?"

"Not exactly my finest hour. Sleeping with a young lady and not following up."

"I didn't ask you to follow up. I didn't follow up, either. I would be the fool of fools telling somebody about that."

"About the fact that you once spent a night with a future president, I don't know. It could be a lucrative story for some tabloid."

Gina shook her head. He truly didn't know her. "I'd rather eat nails," she said, "than to sell any piece of my life to them!"

Dutch smiled. Relieved. *That's my girl*, he wanted to brag.

"So, you gave it up," he said. "Being a public defender, I mean."

"It gave me up," she said.

Dutch frowned. "They fired you?"

Gina nodded. "Yep. As soon as I got back from Miami."

"But you were so devoted, so looking forward to helping the less fortunate. What happened?"

"You remember the guy I drenched in the hotel lounge?"

Dutch nodded. He remembered all of it now. "Yes, of course."

"He filed a complaint. Said I assaulted him for no apparent reason when I threw my drink on him. He didn't press charges, but my superiors said I showed very poor judgment and fired me, anyway. It helped that this attorney I drenched happened to be the grandson of a former superior court judge. So since I was still on probation and they could fire me at will, they did. Summarily."

"You didn't fight it?"

"Did I," Gina said, remembering that wretched time. "I fought it with all I had. I even tried to get in contact with you, since you were the only witness that I felt would tell the truth. I Googled your name."

"But you didn't know my name."

"I knew Walter, I knew your nickname was Dutch, and I knew Boston. So I Googled all three and came up with industrialist Walter Dutch Harber. I called repeatedly but they would never put me through to you. I even went to Boston, to Harber Industries, but they wouldn't even give me an audience with you."

Dutch rolled his cold glass across his suddenly hot forehead. He could feel her pain, could feel it as if it was as much his as hers. But she went on.

"So that's why I founded Block by Block Raiders. I was determined to give voice to the voiceless, because during that time I felt so out of control. I felt like I had no voice."

"Were you angry with me?" Dutch asked her.

"No, sir," she said.

"Bullshit," he said.

She stared in his eyes. "Yes," she admitted. "Very."

"Felt you had given me what I wanted," he said this as he continued to rub the glass against his forehead, as his eyes trailed down the length of her, remembering her in his arms, "then when it was time for you to be helped, I wasn't available."

"It wasn't about that night. That night was on both of us. But when they wouldn't even let me speak to you because I wasn't high enough on some ladder of influence, that was a bitter pill to swallow."

And just like that, after listening to her, after watching her, that powerful connection he felt to her that night in Miami Beach, came flooding back like a tidal wave, and sucked him in. Without thinking about the consequences, without calculating the cost, he reached out and pulled her so firmly into his arms, so protectively, that he sat his glass down and pulled her onto his lap.

The tears that she had been fighting not to shed, came freely for Gina when he pulled her into his arms. And she sobbed openly. She felt so embarrassed that she kept apologizing.

"Don't," Dutch urged her, holding her, handing her his handkerchief. "You don't have anything to apologize for."

She wiped her eyes and looked into his. He smiled, those lines of age showing on the side of his beautiful, kind eyes. "After the awards ceremony, when your assistant told me you wanted to see me, I thought I was being called into the principal's office for punishment," she said with a smile of her own. "Certainly not to tell my life story like this."

Dutch put his hand on the side of her adorable face. "No, that wasn't the reason I called you back here. But I had considered giving you a good spanking."

"Why?" she asked, still smiling. "Because I told you the truth about those budget cuts?"

"You were brutal," he said. "But that's not the only reason."

Gina could see the lust in his eyes. She could feel her own lust rising. "Why else would you want to spank me?" she asked with laughter in her eyes.

He stared at those eyes, and then down at her lips. He began moving toward her lips. "So I can see that tight ass of yours wiggling beneath me," he said, his heat penetrating every inch of her, " when I fuck you again."

As soon as he said those words he put his mouth on hers and kissed her with a jarring kiss. So passionately he kissed her that she clutched onto him in a death grip of an embrace. It had been so long ago, so long forgotten, that now it felt as if they had first made love only yesterday.

He reached inside her pants and her panties and began massaging her mound and then her clit, rubbing softly and then harder and harder, her body jerking with the sensations, her growing wetness thrilling Dutch.

"Oh, *sir*," she said as he massaged her, as those sensations began to pulsate with higher and higher intensity.

But he didn't stop there. With his free hand he reached inside her suit coat and lifted her purple blouse and matching bra. And he began kissing and sucking her breasts, the heat becoming almost unbearable with every lick, every massage, every kiss he seared onto her.

And just as that unbearable heat had him so caught up that he actually considered taking her right on that yellow couch they sat upon, knocks were heard on the door.

Dutch stopped all movement. He had to take a moment first and regain control of his erratic breathing. Only then was he able to help Gina reconfigure her clothing and get off of his lap. Her breasts were still so wet that she feared the saliva would seep through her blouse.

"Yes?" Dutch yelled, able to appear surprisingly calm, it seemed to Gina, considering the tornado they had just been whirled into.

Max Brennan, the man she recognized from TV as the president's best friend and chief of staff, walked into the room.

"Mr. President," he said, his small, tired gray eyes glancing at Dutch, but staring at

Gina. "Sorry to disturb you, sir, but we need to get started."

Dutch stood up, wiping his hands with his handkerchief, and in standing, caused Gina to stand, too. But unlike Dutch, she felt flustered and knew she looked it.

"Is everybody assembled?" Dutch asked him.

"They're assembled in the Situation Room now, sir, yes, sir."

Dutch exhaled, opened his suit coat, and placed his hands inside his pant pockets. He had another long day ahead of him. But when he turned to tell Gina that he had to go, and saw that bewildered look in her eyes, he turned back to his chief of staff. "Give me a moment, Max," he said.

It was obvious to Gina that Max really didn't want to give him another second with her, but he didn't exactly have a choice. He eyed her suspiciously again, as if it was all her fault, and then left back out of the room.

Dutch looked at her. "I have a meeting."

"I understand."

"You understand, don't you?"

"Yes, sir, of course." What Gina didn't understand was why he was wasting time still talking to her. She didn't know a lot about the White House, but she knew enough to know that when they were assembling in the Situation Room, it was serious.

"I want you to have dinner with me tonight," he said to her. It was a spur of the moment thing, something he hadn't even expected to say just a moment ago, but wasn't about to take it back.

Gina was hesitant and it showed.

"You can lobby me some more," Dutch said encouragingly. "I make no promises, however, on what I'll do when that bill hits my desk. But I'll listen to your concerns."

That was at least something, Gina thought, although she also knew that having dinner with him could be bad for her emotional health. Especially the way they were just going at it already. She could only imagine what it would be like tonight. But she couldn't turn down this chance to air her very serious grievances about that budget bill. "What time?" she asked.

Dutch looked upward. "It's probably going to be one of my long days. Christian will come for you, say, around ten? "

Ten at night? That seemed a little late to her. But she wasn't exactly talking about a typical date. "Okay," she said with a nod of assent.

"You wait here. Chris will be in to take you where you need to go." He kept his hand on her arm, however, and began caressing it. "What do you have on your agenda today?" he asked her.

"Lobbying Congress about that dangerous budget bill, what else?"

"Alone?"

"With a friend. I came to DC with a friend."

Dutch studied her. "Your boyfriend?"

Boyfriend? How could he think she'd have a boyfriend the way she was allowing him to kiss on her, to fondle her? "No," she said.

"Husband?"

"No, of course not," she said. "She's female. Her name is LaLa."

"What-what?"

Gina smiled. "Loretta King. She works with me."

"You take care of yourself around this busy town, you hear me?"

"Oh, don't worry about me. I know my way around."

Yes, you do, he wanted to say. But he leaned against her and kissed her on the lips, instead. When he stopped and looked into her eyes, he smiled that smile she was becoming reacquainted with. "I'll see you tonight," he said with a squeeze of her arm, attempting to make clear to her that she won't be sorry, and then headed in that calm, but hurried gait of his, for the Situation Room.

Only Gina felt as if she was the one in a situation.

FIVE

LaLa was right. Nobody in DC wants to be around a loudmouth. That was why, in every congressional office they ventured into, no congressman or woman would see them. They were continually relegated to aides and back-benchers with no pull, who met with them to avoid any backlash for not meeting with them, but with no intention of providing any help or reassurances. The Block by Block Raiders could go to the devil, as far as those congressional staffers were concerned. One, an aide in the office of their very own Congressman Cannon of Newark, said it best: "You insulted the President of the United States, Gina. What did you expect?"

That was the refrain. All day long. What did she expect? Even LaLa got in on the chorus. "It's true, you know," she said as they sat in a café on Capitol Hill to re-think their strategy. They had set aside two days, today and tomorrow, to remain in DC and lobby Congress hard. Now it looked as if they were wasting their time.

"What's true," Gina said, drinking her cappuccino and putting a bright red X next to the name of yet another congressman who wasn't interested in their plight, "is that our doors will have to close sooner rather than later if we can't get some reassurances of no more budget cuts. We could operate, however thinly, on the appropriations from their last round of cuts, and from the donations from the few private sponsors we still have left, but we can't take another hit. For real."

"I know all that," LaLa said. "I'm not talking about that. I'm talking about what happened this morning at the White House, at the awards ceremony."

Gina knew what she meant. She just didn't want to deal with that, especially with what happened afterwards. "What I said was the truth," she said. "I'm not backing down from that. BBR is in trouble because of all of their cuts, and his lack of leadership."

"I know what you're saying, Gina, you know I do. But Fox News ain't looking at it that way. They're playing that tape over and over again as a way to hurt the president. 'Even members of his base hates him now,' is what those reporters at Fox keep saying, playing it up like it's all about how ineffective he's been since he took office."

"And your point is?"

"Your criticism of President Harber has played right into the conservatives' hands."

"Okay, okay. I get it. But I still stand by every word I said."

LaLa looked at her. "And what about tonight?"

Gina hesitated, then looked at her friend. "What about it?"

"You sure that budget bill is all he has in mind?"

Gina declare if LaLa wasn't psychic. Did she see him kissing her today, sucking her breasts, massaging her? Was LaLa hiding in the room? "What in the world else would he have in mind, La?" Gina asked, determined to keep her cool. "He'll meet with me, and then tell the press he gave my grievances a full airing, that's all this invitation is about."

"Nope," LaLa said, shaking her head. "Ain't buying it. No ma'am. If all he wanted to do was to listen to you gab about some budget bill so he can say he met with you, then he would have let that meeting after the awards ceremony do. But no, he meets with you after the ceremony and also invites you to dinner? Nall, girl, LaLa smells a rat in that stew. That man wants to talk to you all right. Pillow talk to you."

"You don't know what you're talking about."

"He's single and you're single," LaLa continued, "so ain't nothing wrong with it. I'm not saying that. But girl, you messing with the sho'nuff big times now if you gonna be messing around with that dude."

Gina frowned, crossed off another congressman's name. "Well I guess I'd better be careful not to mess around with him, then. Right?" she said.

LaLa stared at her. "Right," she said, with little conviction, too.

It seemed like she'd caught this show before. There they were, her and Christian, sitting in the president' private residence at the White House, waiting for what was now nearly two hours, for him to arrive.

"Where is he?" she finally asked Christian, who was seated patiently, as if he was accustomed, in his role as one of the president's personal aides, to waiting. "Is he even here at the White House?"

"Yes, he's here. It's just that things come up."

Of course Gina understood that. But dang. It was coming up on midnight. That man had to be exhausted. "Has he eaten?" she found herself asking before she had a chance to think about it. If she would have thought first, she would have never gotten this personal with the man's aide.

"Probably not," Christian said, his concern showing. "That's one of the things that worry me about him. Sometimes he'll go all day without eating much. Sometimes it gets so bad I have to tell Mr. Brennan about it and he has to get on his case."

"Max Brennan, the president's chief of staff?"

"And best friend, yes, ma'am. He's the only one who can be blunt with the president."

"You can't?"

"Oh, gosh no! He'll fire me in a heartbeat I even think about coming at him like that."

"You mean to tell me he'll fire you for telling him the truth?"

Christian thought about this. "Not for that, exactly. But for disrespecting the office of the presidency. That's real important to him. He doesn't care whether people respect him as Dutch Harber, but he cares an awful lot if they disrespect him as President Dutch Harber. It's all about the office, the representation of the people."

Gina's heart dropped. "Did he feel I disrespected the office when I, to use your phrase, told him off at the awards ceremony?"

Christian didn't want to go there, and especially not with one of the president's females. But this one was turning out to be kind of different. She didn't seem as eager to share her body with the president the way all of the others had, and she'd stand up to him without

82

giving it a second thought. "I don't know if he thought you were disrespectful," he finally said, "but I know it bothered him."

She already knew that much. "And you don't think he's eaten?" she asked Christian.

"I know he hadn't all the times I'd been with him today, and that was up until a couple hours ago, when I went to pick you up."

Gina stood up, causing Christian to stand. "What is it?" he asked her.

"Is there a kitchen around here?"

"A kitchen?"

"Yes. Where they cook food?"

Christian smiled. "But the president has a chef, ma'am."

"I know that, Christian. Work with me, little brother. I thought I'd see what's in the kitchen and whip him up something quick."

Christian looked mortified. "I don't think that's allowed, ma'am."

"I'm not going to poison him! You can watch me the whole time. But you said yourself he probably hadn't eaten all day. That's not good."

"No, it's not," Christian found himself agreeing with her.

"So take me to the kitchen and let's see what we can whip up for him."

Christian was reluctant, more like terrified if you asked Gina, but he escorted her into a small, private kitchen within the residence and watched as she pulled together some kind of pasta/vegetable dish that had him yearning to taste it. She was, in fact, allowing Christian to taste a spoonful when they both looked up and saw the president standing there.

"Sir?" Christian said, mortified. "We were just--"

"We thought you'd be hungry," Gina interrupted. "So *viola*," she said, "we whipped up a dish."

Dutch stood at the doorjamb, his body leaned against it to avoid falling on his face in exhaustion. He could tell that both Christian and Gina were waiting with baited breath. He smiled. "Sounds great," he said, pushing from the door and moving into the kitchen. "I'm famished."

Christian breathe again, and Dutch told him he was excused for the night.

"Hey," Dutch said after Christian left, and he began moving toward Gina.

"Hey yourself," she replied and closed her eyes in anticipation when he leaned over and kissed her on the lips. Then he looked at the food in front of her. "Um," he said, "it smells good."

"Have a seat and try some," she said.

He removed his suit coat, flapped it over the kitchen chair, and took a seat at the small table. Gina found it almost gratifying, this image of the president with his coat over his chair, preparing to eat her food. She only hoped he liked it. Her food always tasted bland to her. But others, like Frank, one of her business associates, for instance, swore by it. She could give those Top Chef contestants a run for their money, he always said.

After preparing a plate for Dutch and one for herself, she sat down at the table, also, Dutch quickly standing slightly until she was seated. Then they bowed their heads, Dutch said a small prayer, and then they began eating. It still didn't taste great to Gina, just

okay, and she kept her eyes on the
president. After a few bites, he looked at her.

"Well?" she said.

He smiled. Then started laughing. His laugh
was so heartfelt that it became contagious, and
Gina started laughing, too.

"What?" she wanted to know. "Is it that
good?"

"No," he said between laughs, "it's
awful. Simply awful." But he couldn't stop
laughing. Gina couldn't either.

"Then why are you laughing?"

"Because," Dutch said, attempting to regain
his composure, "you have balls, lady."

Gina continued laughing, but she didn't get
what he found so funny. "I have balls because
my food is awful?"

"You had the nerve, the *nerve*, to cook for the
leader of the free world – and you can't
cook!" Dutch's laughter went into high gear
again. Gina knew she should have been
offended, but she wasn't. He was being too
honest, and enjoying his honesty, for her to even
think about offense. She laughed, too.

As the laughter began to die down, Dutch exhaled. He'd had his laugh for the month. Then he looked at Gina. His affection for her was immeasurable. And that sudden feeling, that he really liked this lady, caused his once whimsical face to turn dead serious. "Come here," he said to her.

At first Gina was concerned by the change in his demeanor and tone, but she hesitated only briefly, tossed her napkin on the table, and went around to his chair. "Yes?" she said.

He pulled her down onto his lap. Her heart began to pound. "I want to thank you properly," he said.

"Thank me for cooking you a perfectly bad meal?"

Dutch looked at her long, dark neck, her full, titillating lips, her sincere, sexy eyes, and he wanted her here and now. "I want to thank you for thinking of me," he said.

His words touched Gina. She smiled. "What a sweet thing to say."

"I want to do more than say it, Gina." He ran his hand through her soft braids. "Will you let me?"

Her breasts heaved at his touch, something he noticed, too, and just seeing her reaction caused him to react, and not wait for her response. He kissed her. He thought it would be chaste. In his mind he just wanted to feel her lips again. But he couldn't keep it simple, he couldn't keep it chaste. He burrowed into her, kissing her hard and deep and long. When he realized she was willing, and her breasts were becoming hard against his chest, he wrapped her tightly into his arms and kissed her in a fit of passion that left him stunned by his own excitability. He wondered what was wrong with him. He was kissing her as if he was sex starved, as if he hadn't had any in so long that he wanted to kiss her mouth dry.

She could feel his need, and it was mighty, and all she could think to do was to go with it. And she went with it, gladly, wrapping herself into him and experiencing the kind of kissing only he had ever given her. He knew what he was doing, and she loved that he did.

He moved from her lips to her neck, and then her chest, and when he unbuttoned the top buttons on her blouse in a frenzy of passion, and began sucking her breasts in the kind of deep, well schooled suctions, she wanted to jump out of her skin from the intensity of his affection.

He leaned her head back, so that her chest would rise up to him, and he sucked and kissed and moved from breast to breast as if his appetite was as ferocious, as grand as the office he held. This was the leader, and his control, in Gina's estimation, was one more suck away from exploding.

"Oh, Gina!" he said as he lifted her into his arms and carried her out of the kitchen. This was not how Gina had it planned. She had every intention of talking to him and not, under any circumstances, falling prey to his unbridled lust. But it was her lust that she had fallen prey to. Because she wanted him almost as much as he wanted her. This man was amazing, she thought. She'd never felt such a strong, intense need deep within her like this before.

And when he carried her into this huge bedroom, and laid her on the massive bed as if she were the most precious commodity in the world to him, she wanted to cry. She'd had men in her life before, and some were incredible lovers, but she'd only experienced this level of emotion the one time before, when she was with Dutch.

He pulled off both her blouse and her bra, not by loosening them, but by pulling them over her head. Then he lifted her slightly and removed her pants and panties. When he had her naked he stared at her. "Oh my," he said, looking at her bronzed body. And threw off his clothes so fast that Gina thought she could get whiplash watching him. But he was playing for keeps tonight. He dropped those expensive, tailored clothes from his body as if they were scullery rags.

He bent down on his knees at the side of the bed and began kissing her on her stomach, and then turning her over and kissing her buttocks, both cheeks, with a passion that was driving Gina mad with lust. And when he turned her back over, opened her legs, and began licking her and tasting her, she closed her eyes in sheer joy.

And then he stood up. When she opened her eyes, he was staring down at her. His penis was so large and so thick that Gina literally wiped her lips in anticipation of his entry. He just stood there, and began rubbing it, expanding it, as he watched her reaction. Even after he reached in the side table drawer, grabbed a condom and put it on, he still couldn't stop staring at her body, at her face.

"You're so beautiful," he said to her, and he said it in such a way that Gina thought she would scream.

"You aren't bad yourself," she found herself saying, attempting levity, but there was nothing playful in her voice, or his. They were two very serious people. And when he pulled her further onto the bed and he got on top of her, and entered her, she did scream. He was so thick and so long and so juicy that she thought he would explode her.

Dutch thought so, too, as he entered her, as his thick manhood so filled her small passageway that he could feel the mouth of her vagina close onto him like a suction rim. He moved in and out of her, over and over, filling her with so much of himself that tears were appearing in his eyes. He'd never had it so sweet to the feel, so tenderly yet explosively, that he didn't know if he could survive this. And when he came, when his manhood had reached its fill, his entire body shook with the force of a cat-5 hurricane. How could he ever give this up? How could he ever walk away from a lover like her?

Gina was in trouble, too, because her climate was equally as explosive. She tried to contain her joy, she tried to behave like a sister with some sense, but as soon as he drove into her deepest pocket and spilled into her with a throbbing release that shook her to her core, she lifted her body so high to accept the spill that she felt as if she was floating on air.

When they both finally crashed down, and Dutch finally moved off of her, they both lay there, on their backs, staring at the ceiling in the kind of hush disbelief that people experience after an amazing, but traumatic event.

SIX

They just lay there, not knowing what to say, what to do, how to react to something this incredible, when Dutch finally reached out his arm, and pulled her against him. She lay her head on his chest, still reeling.

He looked down at her. He knew there was something special about her when he first saw her a decade ago in Miami. But he never dreamed she could be even more special. This woman had rocked his world again. This was not the way it was supposed to go. He was Wham Bam Harber. And this was supposed to be *thank-you, ma'am* time. But how could he walk away from this?

When she looked up at him, as if she could read his mind, and he saw the sweetness, the decency in her eyes, it took all he had not to pull her on top of him and enter her again. "Are you okay?" he asked her.

"Yes," she replied. "You?"

"I will be." Then he smiled. "You packed quite a wallop, lady."

Gina laughed. She was pleased to know that he felt the earth move too.

"You're like a drug, you know that?" Dutch continued. "Ten years ago, when we hooked up, I hadn't been with a woman in a long time. Had been so busy, you know? But then I had you." He pulled her closer. "And I spent the rest of the last ten years trying to get that high I had with you that night in Miami. I didn't realize that was what I was searching for when I was with all of those women, but now I see it was exactly what I was searching for. And I never got that kind of high again, until tonight, when you allowed me to touch your sweet, tender body and you made me feel so . . . so fortunate."

Dutch had to stop talking. He was actually getting emotional. Gina was stunned too, by how deeply that so-called one night stand affected him.

And then they lapsed, once more, into a companionable silence. Until Gina looked up at him again. "You looked exhausted when you first came home tonight." She made it sound as if he had come to their home, and she was mortified by the implication.

Dutch caught the implication, and it alarmed him on many levels, but he'd sat across negotiation tables with world leaders before. He was an adept at hiding his alarm. "Yes, I was exhausted," he said. "We had one crisis after another one today."

"Is that unusual?"

He smiled. "No." Then he looked at her. "But enough about me--"

"What enough? We haven't even discussed you, except that you looked drained and had to be in crisis mode all day."

"Okay, what do you wish to know?"

"What do I call you?"

"Mr. President," he said.

"Oh. Okay."

Dutch laughed. "My friends call me Dutch," he said. "You had better call me nothing less."

Gina smiled. "Dutch it is. Except in public, right?"

"Correct. It's a question of the office of the presidency. You have to respect the office."

"Understood."

"Now enough about me," Dutch said again. "Tell me about you. I understand cable news is continually running those comments you made earlier today."

Gina shook her head. "I know. I truly hate that they're turning it into some political football. I didn't mean it that way."

"Of course you didn't!" Dutch said as if it was a fact. "But since it bothers you so much now, are you willing to apologize to me?"

This offended Gina. She looked up, to see if Dutch was serious. "Apologize?" she said. "For what? I stand by every word I said."

Dutch stared at her. Then nodded. He had pegged her right. "Good," he said. "I would have been very disappointed in you if you hadn't."

"I feel very strongly about what I said. Those funding cuts to programs like mine have been devastating."

"Block by Block Raiders. As soon as I saw that name on the list of award recipients I thought it an odd one."

"I know. But I kept seeing so many young people in the poorest neighborhoods end up in jail or dead or in such a bleak circumstance that I knew I had to do something. So we help to relocate young gang members who want to start over, or a prostitute who wants a better life, or a drug addict who needs rehab. But first we get their legal house in order because many, if not most of them have major legal issues. And it's not easy. Sometimes we have beg them to accept our help."

Dutch looked at her hair and how soft it was, at her flawless skin and how smooth to the touch he now knew it was. At her long, dark neck. "How does your husband feel about your line of work?"

Gina was amazed. She looked at him. "I'm not married," she said, appalled. "How could you think I'd do something like this and be married?"

Dutch smiled at her wonderful morality. "It was just a question."

"But don't you think it's the kind of question we should have discussed before this, this roll in the hay?"

Roll in the hay, Dutch thought. He'd been on a hay roll or two in his day, and this was no roll in the hay. "My assumption was that you were a single lady, but you never know."

"You mean you haven't investigated me?"

"All of the award recipients were investigated before they were offered the award, to make sure no wanted felons were showing up at the White House. That was enough for me."

"But to answer your question, no, I don't have a husband. And I wouldn't have one who would have a problem with what I do for a living. I'm in the helping profession. That's who I am. I help."

And, to Gina's surprise, he wanted to know all about who she was. And for nearly an hour she told him. About being an only child. About her parents, both school teachers, dying in an automobile accident. About her passion for the poor. "So I got this idea to marry my law degree with my passion for others, and that's how BBR was founded."

"From an idea to a presidential award," Dutch said. "Not bad. Although you turned it down."

Gina felt a little sheepish. She hated that she couldn't have been more magnanimous with him earlier, the way the other award recipients were. But this was business. "Yes, sir," she said. "I couldn't in good conscience allow you to give us an award with one hand, and cut off our funding, our life support, with the other."

"Ah," he said, somewhat sheepish himself. "Thus your disappointment in me."

He said this and looked intensely at her. If he thought she would back down, he was mistaken.

"Yes," she said. "Thus my disappointment."

Dutch pulled her closer against him and kissed her on the forehead. Her honesty, her integrity was refreshing to him. After so many years in politics, he had grown almost jaded by the lack of decency around him. But Gina was different. His only problem, he felt, holding her, was that he wasn't quite sure if her differentness would be an asset at this time in his life, or a liability.

"Miss Lansing," the soft voice of Christian Bale could be heard as Gina slowly began to open her eyes.

When she saw who was standing over her, she frowned. "Christian?" she said. "What are you . . ." Then she realized where she was. "Oh." She sat up on her elbows.

Christian was surprised to see that the president had put her on one of his dress shirts. In times past, with the president's other overnight female guests that Christian had to make this early morning visit to, they were usually still naked.

"It's time to go, ma'am," he said to Gina.

Gina didn't understand. She quickly looked over, fully expecting Dutch to be asleep on the other side of the bed, but he wasn't there. She looked at Christian. "Where's . . ?"

"He's in bed," Christian said.

Gina frowned. "In bed? What do you mean he's in bed? Isn't this his bed?"

Christian hated to admit it. "No, ma'am," he said.

Gina still wasn't understanding. "But . . . I mean. . ." Then she frowned again, as fear began to grip her. "What time is it?" she asked.

"It's seven minutes to five, ma'am."

"Five in the morning? Why are you waking me up at five in the morning?"

"Because," Christian said slowly, "you have to leave before the press starts arriving." He hated this part of his job, and especially with somebody like Gina Lansing. She was gutsy and had heart and the president didn't deserve her.

"So, what you're saying to me is that I can't be seen leaving the White House?"

There was a long pause. "That's correct," Christian admitted. Then he added, as if that would help anything at all: "It's protocol, ma'am."

"Protocol? You mean this is how the president does all of the females who sleep with him, is that the protocol you're talking about?"

Again, Christian hated to admit it. "Yes," he said, to Gina's shock.

She lay there numb. This couldn't be happening. Not after that powerful connection they made last night. How could he let this happen, and happen to *her*? She wasn't one of his booty calls, he couldn't possibly think of her that way after the kind of love making they experienced. She wasn't one of his booty calls!

Or was she?

"Can I see him before I leave?" she asked Christian, her eyes wide with anguish.

"No, ma'am," Christian said succinctly and without hesitation, so there would be no misunderstanding.

In the small hotel room LaLa opened her eyes to the sound of what she thought was a lot of furniture bumping. When she looked over at the bed across from hers, and saw that it wasn't furniture moving around, but Gina, she relaxed.

"Girl, what you doing this time of morning? What time is it?"

"It's six fifteen, and what does it look like I'm doing?"

It was obvious to LaLa that she was packing. The question was why. "You're packing," LaLa said.

"You, young lady, move to the head of the class."

"You're only one year older than me, so don't get ahead of yourself." Then she sat up on her bed, her hands wrapped around her knees. "But for real, Gina, what's going on?"

"We're leaving," Gina said as she threw more clothes into her suitcase.

"Leaving? But I thought we were going to spend the day lobbying some more congressmen."

"What do you mean lobbying more congressmen? Not one would see us yesterday. Not even our own congressman. Except to tell us that he can't see us after the way I supposedly offended the president."

"He said he had a meeting."

"Yeah, right, he was able to spend time with all of his constituents ahead of us, but as soon as it was our turn, he has a meeting. Give me a break. I'm getting out of this town, you hear me? I hate it here! This place is soulless."

"Oh-oh," LaLa said. "It didn't go well with the Flying Dutchman."

Gina, already emotionally drained, stopped packing and plopped down on her bed. "It was awful, LaLa. It was worst than I ever would have imagined."

"What are you saying? He didn't want to talk? He treated you like a whore, what?"

"No!" Gina said, knowing she wasn't making herself clear, but unable to be any clearer. "He was very kind to me. He listened to me for like for an hour straight. I've never met a man who was as attentive to me like that."

"Wait a minute, girl. This ain't making no kind of sense. First you say it was the worst night of your life, now you say he was attentive and kind? You're talking crazy, G!"

"It wasn't the worst night of my life. It was one of the best, actually."

LaLa stared at her friend. "Did he, did y'all, you know . . . sleep together?"

Gina hesitated. There was no use hiding anything from LaLa, she knew her too well. "Yes," she finally said.

"But it was bad, hun? Imagine that big, strapping man don't know how to please a woman."

"It was great. It was fantastic. The best sex I've ever had, and I mean the best."

LaLa frowned. "The best? Please explain yourself. So it wasn't awful?"

"Yes, it was. Not the sex. Not the night we spent together, that was priceless." Then she paused, as a cloud of pain crossed her face. "It was afterwards. This morning."

LaLa's heart dropped. "What happened?"

"I woke up and Christian, that's the young man who picked me up last night, he was standing over my bed."

"He did something to you?"

"No, LaLa! Christian is wonderful, it had nothing to do with him. He was just doing his job. But it was five this morning and he told me I had to leave before the press people started arriving at the White House."

"Makes sense," LaLa said. "They don't want the rumor mill to start churning."

"I know that. I had no problem with that. But it was just that, Dutch, the president, wasn't in bed when I woke up."

"Maybe he's an early riser, maybe he works out, what's the big deal?"

"Christian said he was still asleep. In bed."

"But I thought you said he wasn't in bed?"

"In his own bed."

"Oh," LaLa said when the point dawned. "So he puts you in his love shack, in his make-out room and then leave before you wake up so he don't have to face you in the morning?"

"So it would seem," Gina said, looking away from her best friend in embarrassment. Then she exhaled. "But you know what was the worst part about it?"

"What?"

"When Christian said my leaving was protocol, that President Harber does this all the time, with his different, quote unquote, 'overnight' guests. That made it almost unbearable."

"Oh, Gina! Men are such dogs!"

"Your man ain't no dog. Dempsey ain't like that."

"I know. But he's the exception in my view. And so is Frank, if you're give him half a chance."

"Don't start, La," Gina said, getting back up and continuing to pack.

"That man loves you and you know it."

"Frank and I are friends, and that's all we'll ever be."

"But why? Because Frank's white?"

Gina stopped packing and looked at LaLa. "I just spend the night with the President of the United States, and guess what? He's white, too. How do you sound? Do you ever listen to yourself?"

"Well, whatever. But I still say you should give Frank a chance 'cause it's for damn sure the President of the United States, as you love to call him, ain't giving one to you."

Gina playfully threw a pillow at LaLa and continued to pack. She tried to keep it light, joke it off as if she couldn't care less about that man in the White House. But inwardly, where it counted, she couldn't care more.

SEVEN

A week later, back in Newark, and Gina was doing all she could to stay busy and forget that trip to DC, the awards ceremony, that night with Dutch, all of it, when she heard a car pull up on her drive. She was curled up on her sofa, with her lap top on her lap, her reading glasses on her face, and a coffee mug in her hand, working frantically on yet another grant proposal even though she knew her chances of getting funding for it would be slim to none. Helping gang bangers and drug addicts and hookers were the lowest of the lowest priority in this time of economic crunch. But she still had to try.

When she looked out of the window and saw Frank Rotelli jump from his BMW convertible and hurry towards the porch of her small house, she gave an audible sigh. She didn't know why,

Frank was one of the nicest guys around, a successful corporate accountant who volunteered so much of his time to BBR that some donors assumed he was a staff member. But she always got that eerie kind of queasy feeling whenever he would first appear. Within seconds it would pass, and she would always wonder where did it come from to begin with, but it never failed to come.

"Hey, Frank, what's up?" she said when she opened the door.

"What's up yourself," he said with a grand smile and removed his sunglasses to reveal big, sparkling blue eyes. "Demps told me y'all were back. I just got back from a business trip myself." He looked down the length of her. "I couldn't wait to see you again."

Gina hated when he spoke that way, just hated it, but he always seemed to realize his error and would quickly move on. Which he did this time, too. "The reason why I couldn't wait ," he said, noticing her alarm, "was because I have some good news."

"I could use some good news."

"May I come in?"

Gina really didn't want to deal with him or anybody else right now, but it sounded as if it was business-related, so she let him in.

Her house was neat and clean but extremely small, with a living room so tiny that Frank, the first time he had come over, mistakenly referred to it as her foyer.

"Have a seat," she said as he entered. "Want anything to drink?"

"No, I'm good." He sat down in the chair. She put her laptop on the coffee table and sat on the sofa, tucking her feet underneath her butt.

Frank leaned back with that satisfied, snarky look on his face. He was an attractive man, and he knew how to turn on the charm, but it was a phony, forced charm to Gina. And although LaLa and Demps swore by the man, and wanted desperately for him and Gina to hook up, she wasn't feeling him.

She tried to like him like that, she even went on a couple dates with him, but she finally had to end up telling him what they should have already known: they could be friends, and business associates, but that was all there would ever be between them. Frank agreed easily, as if it was no big deal to him, although Demps later told Gina that she had broken the man's heart.

"So what's the big news?" she asked him when he seemed perfectly content to just sit there smiling and chillin'.

"I know you aren't asking me about big news. I saw you on MSNBC telling President Harber that he could take that award and shove it where the sun don't shine."

Gina was horrified by his characterization. "That's not what I said at all, Frank, why would you say something like that?"

Frank laughed. "It was funny, though, you got to admit that."

Gina failed to see the humor, but she wasn't about to go there with Frank. "So what's up, you said you had some good news?"

"Well, Miss Regina," he finally said, "I do have good news. I've found a brand new sponsor for BBR."

At first Gina was thrilled. They needed every sponsor they could get, which would mean a new infusion of cash. But for some reason her hackles were up. "Who?" she asked him.

"Who?" he said with that nervous smile of his that always made Gina think of a mad man. "Does the 'who' matter?"

"Yes, it matters, Frank. Because I don't want it to be you. You've given all you need to give to BBR. We won't accept any more favors from you."

"That's ridiculous, Gina."

"So you're the new sponsor?"

"My firm, yes."

"No, Frank, no."

"We support many worthy causes every year. Why won't you allow us to support BBR?"

"Because you do support BBR. Your financial advice has been invaluable. Expert financial advice nearly every week, and you don't charge us a dime, are you kidding me? I'm not taking your money, too."

But he wouldn't let up. He talked about how he knew BBR was hurting financially, how that Congress was going to continue to cut programs that help the poor, how she would, in essence, be the fool of fools if she didn't take his money. But Gina took the opposite view. She would be the fool of fools if she took money from a man even her best friend believed was nuts about her.

What saved her from his unrelenting pitch was her cell phone. It began to ring. When she looked at her caller ID and saw that the call was coming from Christian Bale, she excused herself, went into her bedroom that was just off from her living room, and closed the door. Frank, immediately suspicious, stood up.

"Hello, Christian," she said into the phone.

"Hi," Christian said, and then added: "Just a moment."

Frank made his way to her bedroom door, careful not to be heard, and leaned his ear against it. Gina was seated on her bed Indian-style and was leaned forward. She hadn't expected to hear from Christian or anybody related to the president ever again. But now, a week later, Christian calls. To no doubt do Dutch's bidding. She really felt bad for Christian. He was treated more like a pimp than a political aide, it seemed to her.

Christian came back onto the line. "Sorry about that," he said. "I had to give some information to Max Brennan. But how are you, first of all?"

"I'm good," Gina said, "how are you?"

"I was phoning, I'm good, too, but I was phoning because the president is scheduled to be in your city on Saturday night."

There was a pause, as if he was expecting Gina to say something. She simply sat mute. "He's touring some of the more successful urban renewal projects in the city and afterwards he was going to attend a private fund raiser with Mayor Booker, the Governor, and some big money donors from across the state." Another pause. Gina wondered why was he telling her all of this.

"The thing is, Miss Lansing," he finally said, "the president would like for you to come and see him while he's in town."

Nearly a whole week and not a word from him. He comes to town for some fundraiser and expects her to drop everything and go and see him? "Sorry, no, I can't make it."

"I can pick you up around ten," Christian said, as if she had accepted wholeheartedly.

"I said no, Christian, I can't make it."

"You have to make it, ma'am."

"Ex*cuse* me?" Gina said, astounded by his comment. "Why do I *have* to make it?"

"Because he's the President of the United States and he's asking you to. You have to make it, ma'am."

Gina closed her eyes. What on earth had she gotten herself into? She had slept with the President of the United States. The president! She opened her eyes. "Did he say what it is he wants to see me about?" As if it wasn't as obvious as the nose on her face.

Even Christian hesitated on that one. Sex, *duh*, she could imagine him saying. "No, ma'am," he said, instead. "He didn't say."

Gina felt trapped. Any other man and she would have told him what he could do with his invitation. But it wasn't any other man they were talking about. It was the President of the United States, a man who had the power to veto any legislation that would defund the very program that was her life blood. Besides, Christian was right. You don't say no to the president. "I'll see," Gina decided to say. "Call me back Friday morning. I'll let you know if I can make it." And she clicked off.

When it was clear to Frank that the call was over, he hurried back down into the living room. He had been only able to hear her side of the conversation, but that was enough to anger him nearly beyond reason. And although, when she returned to the living room, he smiled and continued to convince her how foolish she was not to take his money, inwardly he raged.

"*That bitch*!" he kept saying to himself. "*Out of my sight one night, she spent just one night in DC, and already spread her legs for some joker! Probably some Mandingo nigger with a dick longer than a gotdamn telegram pole! That's what she likes. That's why she won't bother with me. I'm not good enough for her, not big enough for her. But that's cool, that's all right. I'll get mine. And when I get finished with her the last thing on the face of this earth she's going to want is some dick, Mandingo or otherwise!*"

And he kept smiling, kept trying to convince her that BBR needed all the financial backing it could get and his firm was willing and more than able, while he kept inwardly calling her a bitch, over and over, like a mantra.

Block by Block Raiders was a large, converted warehouse on a dead-end street. The staff consisted of eighteen workers, mostly social workers and counselors, with half in the field and the other half in the office doing the paperwork that would get a gang banger relocated away from his community, or a prostitute a legitimate job, or a drug addict some treatment. Any legal issues, and there were usually many, were referred to Gina or Dempsey.

The board of directors, Gina, LaLa, Dempsey Cooper and Frank Rotelli, were in the office in the back, seated around a conference table, reviewing the organization's financial records. It wasn't a pretty sight. Their private donations were so few that the dollars just weren't there.

"How long?" Gina asked and everybody looked at Frank.

Frank pinched the bridge of his nose and then looked up, revealing tired, blue eyes. "Two months, three if we're lucky."

LaLa was astounded. "That's *all*? Damn!"

Gina was astounded too, but she was more interested in answers. "Any word from the Crader Foundation, Demps?"

Dempsey was LaLa's old man, a handsome, smart, corporate attorney who was also their best fundraiser. "Yes, there's a word, and the word is still no."

Gina leaned her head back in frustration. Frank stared admiringly at her long neck.

Demps rubbed the top of his low-cut fade. "It's just a fact of life these days, Tor," he said. "Everybody's broke. They want to give, they just don't have it to give anymore."

"And if the president doesn't veto that appropriations bill, we're done for," LaLa said. "For real this time."

Earlier, exactly one week and one day after Gina laid in bed with Dutch Harber and told him about that very budget bill, it squeaked through the House of Representatives largely on a party line vote. The Senate had already passed the measure. Now it was up to Dutch.

"Is the bill still in conference?" Frank asked Gina.

"Yup," LaLa answered. "Once the House and Senate versions are reconciled then it goes to the president's desk. Which means," LaLa added, looking at Gina, "the president is our last hope. Our only hope, really."

Demps, too, looked at Gina. She had told LaLa about that phone call from Christian, and the invite for Saturday night, and LaLa had told Demps. They both came over to Gina's house that night and made a special plea for her to go see the president and lobby him hard. If he vetoed that bill and sent it back to Congress, they still stood a fighting chance. If he passed it, they were doomed.

"We're doomed," Demps said now as he had that night, "if President Harber doesn't see the light."

She arrived at the hotel that Saturday night in a limousine with Christian. And the ruse was on. The decision apparently had been made that he would pretend that she was his date. He even put her arm on his and walked her through the lobby of that fancy palatial hotel as if nothing in this wide world was wrong with that. The fundraiser was being held in the ballroom of the hotel, and the president, Christian said when he deposited her in the penthouse suite, would be with her shortly.

Gina was ready for him this time. She wasn't about to take this cruel treatment lying down. If she gave him her body, what would she get in return? That was how they did it in Washington, wasn't it? One hand washes the other one? You scratch my back, I'll scratch yours? She was loaded for bear. If she was to sleep with him, she was leaving with his commitment to veto any budget proposal that included cutting funds to programs like hers. Simple as that.

Only it wasn't that simple, Gina thought as she sat on the sofa of the luxuriously appointed room. She was reducing herself to the president's whore. Yeah, that would make her a high class whore, certainly higher than she was back in Miami before his foray into politics, but still a whore.

Tears came to her eyes as she realized her life pattern. After her parents died, she felt as if her education was all she had. And she put her everything into it. But on her first real job, as a public defender, she was fired before she even got started good. All because she wouldn't prostitute herself to some young, hot shot attorney with connections. Then she turned to BBR. It became all she had. And now, once again, she had to prostitute herself to save it. Although she knew, deep down, that it would be taken from her, too.

She stood quickly, and hurried for the front door. She couldn't do this. She couldn't allow herself to have to go down this dark, dingy road. She would beg every business she could find, plead with every foundation that would see her, before she allowed herself to become somebody's whore. Even the president's whore.

She could hardly believe that she had even come. Dutch Harber wasn't interested in anything but her body. That was why he didn't invite her to the hotel fundraiser as his guest, but to his hotel room, as his whore. All of her life she had to deal with this. Never quite good enough. Everybody else gets to walk through the front door, she gets in through the rear.

She flew open the door of the suite and ran out of the room, determined to never be so desperate again, and she ran right smack into a tall, steel frame. When she looked up, she realized the President of the United States, the leader of the free world, was holding her in his arms.

EIGHT

He handed her a glass of wine, and then sat on the sofa beside her. Not a word had been spoken since he brought her back into his suite from the corridor, other than assuring the secret service, who had begun to move in when Gina first ran out, that there was no threat at all. He unbuttoned his suit coat, this one a light brown, and crossed his legs.

He looked at her in full. He had missed her terribly. But his days began early and ended, oftentimes, after midnight, especially with so many critical issues on his plate. And besides, he still wasn't certain that any of this, some major relationship, would be in the best interest of either one of them. But he missed her terribly and knew he wasn't about to come to her hometown and not feast his eyes on her again. Where it was headed, he didn't know.

"Where were you going in such a hurry?" he asked her.

"Why wasn't I invited to the fund raiser?" Gina asked him. She wasn't playing any games with him tonight.

"I didn't know you were interested in an invite."

"You didn't know if I was interested in some roll in the hay in your hotel room, but you asked me anyway. Or, correction, your flunky asked me." She hated referring to sweet Christian by such a name, but seeing Dutch again, looking so gorgeous and so full of himself, a man who never in his life had to degrade himself to get anything, and she was getting angry.

Dutch sipped from his wine. He could see her anger, could feel it. "I prefer to keep my private life private," he said. "Allowing my woman to be seen at a fund raiser would only feed the gossip mill and I've got enough on my plate than to add another course."

"Your woman?" Gina said.

"That's what I said," Dutch said, although he wasn't certain why he'd said it. They hadn't established anything yet. But seeing her again made him suddenly feel a sense of possession, of protectiveness.

"For a minute there," Gina said, "I thought you were going to say your whore, because that's exactly how I feel."

Dutch frowned. "My whore?" he said. "Don't you ever call yourself that! Why would you say such a thing, Gina? How could you say such a thing?"

If he didn't know that, Gina thought, she certainly couldn't school him. "That's how I feel," she admitted.

Dutch quickly sat his glass of wine on the table behind the sofa, and moved over to Gina. His face looked so serious, so alarmed that he began to alarm her. "Oh, sweetheart," he said, putting his hand on the side of her face, "why would you feel like that?"

"Why?" Gina asked, amazed he didn't know. "You make passionate love to me and send me on my way. I don't hear from you for an entire week, an entire week, and then you phone, Christian phones, and invites me, not to have dinner with you, not to attend the fundraiser with you, but to have sex with you."

"To have sex. . . Chris didn't put it that way."

"He didn't have to. Your invitation put it that way. Come, not to eat, not to party, come to go to my hotel room."

"I wanted to see you again. I can't come to your house, and you know as well as I that going out in public would only invite the kind of scrutiny neither one of us need right now. I'm still, we're still trying to figure this out." He studied her. Unsure now more than ever if she could handle the scrutiny when it eventually came. "You do understand that. Don't you?"

Gina looked at him. She was blown away by how serious he looked. "I understand, but--"

"No buts, Gina. You have got to understand that. This isn't just some relationship. I can't take you to the club or out to dinner on a whim. We're considering a relationship while I'm still president. You have to understand what that means."

Oddly enough, it wasn't until he said it, did she understand it. On some level she already had, but in her heart she had no clue. She nodded, felt surprisingly relieved somehow. "I understand," she said.

"Since last week, after our night together, I haven't thought about any other woman but you. But we've got to be cautious here. You have got to understand what you're getting yourself into if we decide to go down this road. I probably shouldn't have ordered Chris to call you. You don't need this life, trust me, you don't. But I had a moment of selfishness and told him to make the call, anyway. I'm sorry."

He apologized so heartfelt that Gina felt like the villain. Which astounded her. "I was just wondering what happened," she said. "I thought we had made a connection."

"We did. Of course we did. But there's so much more we have to consider."

"I know you're a public person, Dutch, I understand what you're saying. But I knew that when I, when we slept together, I knew that going in."

Dutch continued to study her. If she only knew what she was getting into, what life in a fishbowl was really like, she'd run away from him as fast as her feet could propel her. He tried to keep her at bay, a sweet girl like her didn't need this aggravation. He tried for an entire, agonizing week. Every day he thought about her, every night he wanted her in his bed, filling her with his love. But she didn't need this.

But he told Chris to phone her, anyway. His only solace was that she would at least have some general idea of what life would be like under the microscope. She, after all, lobbied Congress enough to have some idea about life in DC. But now he was beginning to wonder if she had even grasped the general notion. She had intellectually, he was confident that she understood theoretically. But on an emotional level, he wasn't so sure.

He placed her glass on the back table and moved closer to her. He put his arm across her shoulder and pulled her to him. "Let me hold you," he said, wrapping her into a bear hug. He closed his eyes as he held her, as he thought about how badly he wanted her, maybe even needed her, and he thought about how tough this journey would be for her, for both of them.

He pulled back slightly, and looked at her. She opened her closed eyes too, and looked at him. His breath caught at the beauty, the humanity he saw in her eyes.

"You can run now, you know," he said with a smile that seemed to Gina to be more regretful than joyous.

"I know," she said.

"You can tell me now that this is not for you and I'll leave you alone forever, Gina, I promise you I will."

Her throat almost constricted at the thought of never feeling his touch again, of never seeing his face or those lines on the side of his eyes up close and personal again. "I know," she said.

"It will be brutal, honey, you understand that?"

Why was he harping on that again, she wondered, and looking so concerned about it? "I told you I did, Dutch."

"They may bring up your time as a public defender, and the fact that you were fired." He looked her squarely in the eye. "Including what happened that led to the firing, and who you may have been with."

Gina's heart dropped. "But how will they know, about who I was with that night I mean? You didn't tell anyone?"

Dutch frowned. "Of course I didn't tell anyone. But the scrutiny is the point, Gina."

"And I'll deal with the scrutiny. I was fired, yes, I was. But I don't see why anybody would judge me based on what happened a decade ago."

He rubbed her hair, and her back. "I know, sweetie, I know," he said. "I'll never judge you, not ever." He exhaled. "But I just want you prepared when others do. And they will, I don't care how trivial, because people can be vicious, Gina. They can tear you down with glee in their eyes. They can't take it, nobody really can, but they can easily dish it."

Gina leaned her head against the arm he had around her shoulder and he looked at her. The droopiness of one of her eyes made her look so sexy to Dutch at that very moment that he felt as if she was his already. But he contained himself.

"You take it, Dutch," she said. "All of that crap they write about you, I mean."

"I take it, yes, but that doesn't mean it doesn't hurt. I'm still a human being, I have a thick skin, but I'm still a human being. And some people are so judgmental and hateful that it'll stun you just like it stunned me when I first entered politics. I mean they are vicious. They know what's right and how it's done and everybody else is a fool, that's how they think. Of course they're the real fools for being so absolute about another human being, but I just want to prepare you." As if anybody could be prepared for what she could face, he thought. And again the ever-growing guilt that always came whenever he thought about the fact that he was about to thrust her into the blinding lights with him, gnawed at him.

Gina saw the guilt in his eyes. She ran her fingers through his soft, black hair. "Don't worry about me," she said with a wry smile, "I can take care of myself. Been doing it since I was fifteen, matter of fact."

"Oh, yeah," Dutch said, staring into her eyes, lifting her braids up and dropping them back down, loving the way the up-do highlighted her high cheekbones. "You ain't so tough. Know how I know?"

"How?" she asked. He was closer now, her body nearly on his lap.

He moved even closer to her face, staring at her mouth. "Because you aren't tough enough to stop this," he said and pressed his lips onto hers.

He began kissing her, in a soft, delicate delight. He didn't want to rush. He'd been wanting this since the last time he had it, and he didn't want to rush. Gina leaned back and enjoyed every minute of his passion, her mouth moving in circular rhythm to his, her body growing more tense the longer he kissed her.

And when he lifted her up and carried her to the bedroom, she felt as if she was burning with fire. He laid her on bed and they began undressing him, tossing his clothes aside. And then he was going after her, desperate to see her beautiful brown naked body again. And when he did, when they were both naked, he began kissing her breasts, her stomach, her thighs, and then her womanhood. He lapped it up, making her so wet that she was hunching her back in anticipation. He looked up at her. There would be no condom this time.

He moved up to her and entered her, his erection so stiff it felt like an actual rod entering her. "Oh," she yelled out as he entered her, moving in so deep, so expertly as only he knew how. And the thought of not rushing, of taking it slow and easy, became a fairytale, because he could not contain himself any longer and began to pound.

He pounded her with all the strength he had in him, and the enjoyment wouldn't ebb, wouldn't let up, wouldn't give him a moment's respite. It felt so good, the fierceness of it, and he couldn't stop pounding her. He turned her over, entered her from the back, and continued to gyrate. Gina held onto the bedspread, but it was a flimsy hold, as her entire body kept slipping down to him, kept being sucked in by that wonderful feeling he and only he had been able to give to her.

And when the release came, it didn't seep out like a drip, but shot out like a sieve, stretching every muscle in her body as she took him in. And he kept pounding. Until he screamed her name and poured out his last gush that drained him of all, every solitary ounce, of his energy.

He collapsed on top of her.

Gina thought it was a dream. That kind of sex couldn't possibly be true. And then she heard her name. *Miss Lansing. Miss Lansing.* But why would Dutch call her Miss?

She opened her eyes. Her environment seemed so strange. Until she remembered. Hotel. Fundraiser. Dutch. She smiled at the thought of Dutch. Was that his hand touching her? She looked up, at the man standing beside her bed. Only it wasn't Dutch. It was Christian. And that look on his face made clear to her that she'd been left again. She didn't ask this time, but quickly looked to the other side of the bed. The indentation where Dutch's body had been was still there. But he was gone.

She laid her head back.

"I'm sorry, Miss Lansing," Christian said.

"Call me Gina."

"The president would prefer I call you Miss Lansing."

"Oh, he would, would he?" Gina was so disgusted with herself, with Dutch, that she didn't know what to do.

"There's no rush, ma'am. I'll just wait in the lobby until you're ready."

"What time is it?"

"It's four after nine, ma'am. Sunday morning."

She couldn't believe she slept this long. Then again, she could. Dutch had her in his arms all night, and she felt safe and protected and so comfortable. "I take it the president is in a different suite? That this wasn't his suite, after all."

"This was his suite, ma'am. He's not in a different suite. He's gone."

Gina looked at Christian. "Back to Washington?"

Christian shook his head. "He has to tour the tornado damage in Oklahoma and then the flood damage in Tennessee. So he won't have a moment to spare, or be back in Washington until probably well after midnight tonight, ma'am. He had to get an early start, so he didn't want to wake you."

"That's bullshit and you know it!"

Christian corrected himself. "He felt it best he didn't wake you."

That's more like it, Gina thought. As if he was so afraid she might want something from him, like a thumbs down on that budget bill. And he didn't even want to discuss it. She came to discuss it, and it never came up. She felt like an abject failure. And LaLa and Demps and all of their employees were depending on her.

Or was his motives more personal? Had all of that talk about preparing her a ruse to get her into bed, and then he pulled his disappearing act again? Was this supposed to make clear to her that he didn't want her, just her body? And only when that was convenient for him? He was, after all, the president. Who was she to complain?

Well, to hell with him, she thought, and moved to get out of bed. Until she realized she was still completely naked.

She looked at Christian, who looked thoroughly contrite. "Will you excuse me so I can get dressed?"

"Yes, ma'am. But . . ."

"But what?" She didn't see where it would be up for debate.

"I know you're upset with the president, ma'am, and you should be. I thought it was a . . . bad move on his part leaving you like this."

"Did you share that opinion with him?"

"Oh, no ma'am, I couldn't. I mean, I can't just. . . He's the president, ma'am."

"And that gives him a license to treat people any way he pleases?"

"No, of course not," Christian said, trying him best to be reasonable. "But, he left me behind to make sure you were okay and that you got home safe. That's why he made me stay here in Newark. He'd never done that before."

Gina frowned, stared at Christian. "Never done what before?"

"He's never, after, I mean---"

"What you mean to say is that after he's fucked other women in the various hotels of the various towns where he's appeared in the past, he's never asked you to see them safely home. Is that what you mean, Chris?"

Christian swallowed hard, his hands clutched together in front of him. She was so blunt, he thought, and so right on. "Yes," was all he could manage to say.

"And I'm supposed to feel privileged by the fact that he left an escort for me?"

Christian wanted to be anywhere but here. "Yes," he said truthfully again.

"Like hell," Gina said. Then she frowned disgustedly. "I'll meet you in the lobby," she said.

"He's not like that," Christian blurted out, his blue eyes wide with apprehension. Gina looked at him. "I mean, yes, he's dated a lot of women, if you can call it dating. He's a bachelor who's been in the public eye for eight straight years, five as a United States Senator and three now as president, and he has to pick his moments. I mean, with respect, Miss Lansing, who do you think you're dealing with? You had to know this wouldn't be a regular kind of relationship, not with Dutch Harber, you had to have known that. Didn't you?"

Gina stared at Christian. She knew it would be a different kind of affair, she knew that going in. But that still didn't give Dutch license to treat her as if she was that one-night-stand he banged in Miami. She'd never accept that.

"I'll meet you in the lobby," she said to Christian.

"Yes, ma'am," Christian said, and left.

NINE

Monday morning and Gina was late for work. She walked into BBR headquarters after eleven am, three hours off of her normal schedule. She wore shades to cover up her tired eyes, and carried her briefcase and a cup of coffee. LaLa was waiting for her, sitting behind her desk in the office they shared, and Dempsey was seated on the edge of the desk.

"Where in the world have you been?" LaLa asked as soon as she walked in. "And why didn't you turn on your cell phone?"

Gina had a headache out of this world and really didn't want to hear it. After that experience Saturday night, where she gave it up to Dutch, once again, and didn't even get a chance to so much as mention that appropriations bill that now sat on his desk, she was too disgusted with herself to even call her friends. And facing them today, with all of the questions she knew they had, was almost unbearable.

"Good morning to you, too," she said as she moved over to her desk and sat herself and her briefcase down. She grasp hold of her cup of coffee with both hands and began sipping it.

"You look awful," Dempsey said.

"Thanks a lot."

"I mean drained, tired. That's all I meant, Gina. When you should be celebrating."

Gina stared at Dempsey and LaLa. They looked so cheerful. They actually thought she had convinced Dutch. They were actually expecting her to bust out with some big news. Her heart dropped. "And why should I be celebrating?" she asked him.

"Haven't you heard?" LaLa asked.

"Heard what?"

LaLa smiled, looked at Dempsey. "I told you she didn't know."

"Know what, LaLa? What is it?"

LaLa sat up straight in her chair. "Well, whatever you did to that man Saturday night,

141

girl, it worked Monday morning because our
President Walter "Dutch" Harber has vetoed the
appropriations bill."

Gina snatched her shades off of her
face. "You lyin'!"

"He vetoed it and sent it back to Congress!"

Gina smiled and leaned back in her
chair. "Really?"

"You mean you didn't know?" Dempsey asked
her. "He didn't tell you he was going to do it?"

Gina shook her head. "No, he didn't tell me
anything. We didn't even discuss it."

"Didn't discuss it?" LaLa asked,
confused. "Then what the hell did you meet
with him for if you didn't discuss it?"

Gina's desk intercom buzzed. *Saved by the
bell*, she thought. "Yes, Al?"

"A Mr. Herbert Montescue is here to see you,
Tore."

Gina looked at LaLa puzzled. LaLa was puzzled
too. "Send him in," Gina ordered. "Who's
Herbert Montescue?" she immediately asked.

"Hell if I know," LaLa replied.

The office door opened and a tall, well-built man in his mid-forties entered. "Regina Lansing?" he asked as he walked toward her.

"Yes," Gina said as she stood to her feet. "And this is my business associates, Loretta King and Dempsey Cooper."

"Miss King, Mr. Cooper, nice to meet you."

"Have a seat, Mr. Montescue."

"Thank-you," Montescue said cheerfully as he sat in front of Gina's desk. Gina also sat down. "I know you're wondering why I'm here, so I'll be short and sweet and to the point. I'm a businessman from Tennessee, a friend of a friend of yours."

"And who's this friend?" LaLa asked him.

Montescue looked to his side. He smiled at LaLa but addressed Gina. "Dutch Harber," he said in a lowered tone.

Gina glanced at LaLa. "Go on," she said.

"Well, Dutch and I were talking yesterday, he was in Tennessee taking a look at that awful flood damage along the Cumberland. Well he pulled me aside and we got to talking, just general conversation you understand, and he mentioned some worthy causes around the

country that he found interesting. No
endorsements of any sort, mind. No
endorsements at all. But interesting, he
said. They were interesting causes that he
personally found interesting. Such as Block by
Block Raiders, for example." He looked directly
at Gina when he said this.

"And what exactly did he find interesting
about BBR?" LaLa asked. She didn't like
Montescue. He spoke in riddles.

"Perhaps I can speak with you alone, Miss
Lansing?"

"No, it's okay," Gina said. "She's okay. So, if I
understand you correctly, you decided to check
out our organization because we won the
Mountain Movers award?"

"Exactly," Montescue said in a relieved
tone. Dutch was right, he thought. She is
sharp. "And so I wish to donate," he said, pulling
out his checkbook, "to this worthy cause."

Gina's heart began to soar. She glanced at
LaLa, who was holding her breath.

"If that's all right with you?" Montescue
asked.

"Yes," Gina said, working hard to contain her elation. "All donations are appreciated."

Montescue wrote the check and then ripped it from his checkbook, handing it to Gina. Then he immediately stood up. "Well, I'd better get back," he said. "As I stated earlier, I, too, found your organization here interesting and thought I'd do my part." He extended his hand. "You have a wonderful day, Miss Lansing," he said.

"You too, Mr. Montescue. And thank-you so much."

"Oh, don't thank me," he said, placing his checkbook back inside his suit coat pocket. "I'm just privileged to be a friend of your friend. Oh, and of course, I have other like-minded friends who would be very interested in a program such as yours. Perhaps they can likewise get in touch?"

"Yes, by all means," Gina said. "We would be most appreciative."

Montescue smiled. Looked Gina up and down. She wasn't the sort he would have thought a man like Dutch Harber would find attractive, but for some odd reason, he could see absolutely why he'd find her attractive. "Goodbye, Miss Lansing." He looked toward Dempsey and LaLa. "Miss King, Mr. Cooper."

Then he walked out.

After he walked out, Dempsey and LaLa hurried to Gina's desk. Gina finally looked at the check amount.

"It better not be in the hundreds," LaLa said. "Not if the president ordered him to do it."

"The president can't order him to do any such thing," Dempsey said. "That would be illegal."

"That check ain't illegal though, is it?" LaLa asked Dempsey.

"No," Dempsey assured her. "I mean, what's to stop a friend of the president's from donating to an organization run by another one of his, quote unquote, 'friends'?"

"How much is it, Tore?" LaLa asked in great anticipation.

Gina looked at her best friend, speechless.

"What?" LaLa anxiously wanted to know.

Gina swallowed hard. "Four hundred and fifty-five thousand dollars," she said.

Dempsey snatched the check from her hands to see it with his own two eyes.

LaLa fainted.

Two hours later, when her day couldn't get any better, it actually did. She was in Cribb's, a sports bar they often frequented for lunch, with a now fully recovered LaLa, Dempsey, and Frank, when her cell phone began to ring. They were celebrating, not just the major donation, their biggest private donation ever, one that would keep the doors open until Congress got its act together. But they were also celebrating the fact that Dutch had vetoed that appropriations bill. When she looked at her Caller ID and saw that it was Christian, she excused herself and hurried through the bar's exit.

"Hey, Christian," she said once she stepped outside, "tell Dutch great move."

"Why don't you tell me yourself," Dutch replied on the phone. He was in a limousine on his way to visit wounded troops at Walter Reed.

Gina was astounded to hear that it was his voice, and not Christian's. "I didn't think you were allowed to talk on telephones."

"Oh, yeah," Dutch replied, "and why's that?"

"Saturday night together," she said, remembering how hard he pounded her. "No phone call whatsoever on Sunday."

"Didn't have a moment's free time on Sunday." Dutch remembered, too. Remembered how she arched that fabulous brown body up to his as his dick slid deeper into her.

"No free time," Gina said, "except to pull certain businessmen aside and sing the praises of BBR. Of which I also thank-you."

"All of the award winning organizations are worthy causes." He said this so formally that Gina realized she had to check herself. What Montescue did for BBR had to have no direct connection to him.

"I agree," she said.

"I've arrived at my destination so I've got to run," he said as the limo eased to a stop. "Have dinner with me Friday night."

Gina was immediately hesitant.

"I would prefer sooner," Dutch went on, "but with my super-hectic schedule it can't be any sooner."

"You work too hard," Gina found herself

saying. "I used to always think that when I'd see you on television."

"You're correct. But it goes with the territory. A car will meet you at the airport. Chris will phone later with more details, but I've got to run."

"But wait a minute," Gina said, panic seeping through her. "I haven't said yes."

"Then say it." She'd never know it, but Dutch was holding his breath.

Gina rubbed her forehead. Why she was always allowing herself to be suckered like this, she'd never know. "Yes," she said.

He smiled relief. "Chris will phone. Take care of yourself."

"You too."

And just like that, what she thought was off and off forevermore, was on again.

TEN

Christian was in the limo that met her at the airport and the ride to the White House was a relaxing one. Unlike that night at the hotel in Newark, or even their "meeting" that night after the awards ceremony, Gina didn't feel the anxiety or pressure she used to feel. Getting that bill vetoed certainly helped, especially when one of the reasons for the veto Dutch cited was that he would not sign a bill that balanced the budget on the backs of the poor and middle class without balancing revenues on the top earners as well. And Herb Montescue's big check helped, too.

"What are you thinking?" Christian asked her. He somehow felt a sense of comradeship with Gina. He'd seen women come and go at the White House, but he'd never seen the same woman come as many times as Dutch had Gina coming. Which pleased him mightily. Of all of Dutch's females, there was something about this one that seemed so promising to him.

"I was just realizing an awful truth," Gina replied.

Christian looked at her. "What awful truth?"

"That I've been so concerned about the future viability of BBR, that it's commanded almost all of her time. Now that we have more donors and we're turning that corner, I feel as if a burden's been lifted and I can now get on with my life. Sounds crazy?"

"No, ma'am, not at all."

"Christian, why do you call me ma'am? How old are you?"

"Twenty-five, ma'am."

"Well I'm only thirty-five so it's not like I'm ancient either."

"I understand that, ma'am, I mean. . . The president would be highly upset if I treated you with any less respect."

Gina looked at Christian. This may be a unique chance to get a better read on

Dutch. "The way you describe him he seem so stern and rigid. Is he really like that?"

"No, ma'am, but, I mean, he's the president." He said this as if that explained it all, and then looked, once again, out of the window.

Gina leaned back. Dutch had warned her that this was another world she would be stepping into, and she had better understand that. But now she wondered if she understood a thing about this new world.

The limo stopped at a side portico at the White House and Gina prepared to get out. She wore a sleek aqua and white dress, black stilettos with just a splash of aqua, and a gold scarf around her neck. Her braids were in an up-do that highlighted the beautiful contours of her face. When Christian first saw her he thought she looked angelic, and told her so. When the door to the limo opened and, to her surprise, she didn't have to get out because Dutch got in, she could see that same admiring look in his eyes that she had seen in Chris's.

As soon as Christian got out of the limo and the doors were closed, Dutch pulled her into his arms, kissing her as he did. He was literally moaning as he kissed her, and Gina wondered more than once if the driver could hear him. When they separated, although he kept her in his arms, he looked at her, at her hair and her face, and smiled. "You're a wonderful addiction, lady, you know that?"

"You've mentioned it before," Gina said with a smile of her own, taking her hand and touching the lines on the side of his gorgeous green eyes. He looked tired and drained to her, but exuberant too. As if he was going to take this break from all of his worries and make the absolute most of it.

And they were off, driving to Mirth, a restaurant not that far from Washington Avenue, and one she'd never ventured into. She didn't realize they were a part of a convoy of cars and SUVs until she and Dutch stepped out. There were no cameras waiting to flash, because this was not an officially announced event for the president, causing the press to have to scramble. But it was clear to Gina when they entered by a back entrance at the restaurant that the secret service had done its job. An entire private section of Mirth had been condoned off just for the two of them.

After a wonderful meal and great Champagne, they made their way back to the White House residence. To Gina's delight, he didn't take her to his "love shack" or whatever bedroom name he had for it, but into another large bedroom that looked more lived-in, more comfortable than the previous room.

"What's this?" Gina asked him as they entered the large room. "The infamous Lincoln bedroom?"

"No, it's my bedroom," Dutch said, closing the door. "At least while I occupy this residence." He sat on the bed, removing his shoes.

"So that bedroom I slept in before, the one I thought was yours, wasn't?" She asked this as she walked leisurely around the room, running her hand along the furniture as she walked. She already knew the answer, but she needed to hear what he had to say.

Dutch considered her. Christian had told him how much the fact that she had not slept in his bed had hurt her. "No," he said, unloosening his tie. "It wasn't." Then he added: "No woman has ever slept in this room with me."

Gina leaned against the dresser, folding her arms. "Not even Kate Marris," she said.

Dutch hesitated, surprised that she even knew about his ex. "How would you know about that?" he asked her.

"Google, my brother," Gina said.

Dutch snorted. "I hope *Google* also told you that we're no longer together. But yes, not even her." After he removed his tie, his arms kind of fell down to his lap in an exhaustive flap-down, and his body leaned slightly forward.

"Whoa," Gina said, hurrying to his side. "Are you all right?"

"I'm okay," he said, nodding. Gina sat beside him, her hand on his strong shoulder that was now slumped. He smiled at her, but the tiredness in his eyes told a different story.

"You work too hard," she said. "And then to have to take me to dinner when we could have just as easily stayed here and let me cook you a meal."

Dutch couldn't help it. He didn't have the energy for laughing, but he laughed anyway.

"Why you laughing?" Gina asked, trying to conceal her own smile.

"The idea of eating another one of those meals of yours," Dutch said, shaking his head, "I'm sorry, honey, but that's laughable."

Gina grabbed one of his pillows off of his bed and clobbered him with it. "That is so not funny," she said, as he fell back on the bed laughing.

He looked so gorgeous to her at that very moment, with his silky black hair all tousled and dropped down into his gorgeous face, that she found herself staring at him.

His laughter died when he realized she was looking at him so lovingly. He'd seen it before, many times before, from various females that had come and gone in his life. But with them, when they gave him that *he'll do nicely* look, he felt burdened. With Gina, he felt honored.

He took her by the arm and pulled her down beside him, laying her head on his chest. He closed his eyes. There was no human being on earth he would rather be with than Gina, and the thought of it, that his feelings for her were intensifying, gave him some pause. When he lost his fiancée in that plane crash, and his father, he found love to be a disagreeable, unreliable nuisance that caught you at your highest peak and lowered you to your lowest depths. Love, to him, became too risky and he had vowed to never bother with it again. Not all-out the way he had loved Caroline, the way he had loved his father.

And now Gina comes along. Young, vibrant, smart and wonderful. Everything he wanted and, if truth be told, needed. And he cared about her in a way that was beginning to disturb him. He had so much going on, too much already, and to fall in love right smack in the middle of his presidency, when Republicans were doing all they could to tear that presidency down and Democrats were sitting on their lazy rears doing nothing to prop it up, would be insanity.

And the idea of putting Gina through this, he thought, as he began rubbing her soft, braided hair. He wasn't at all sure if she could handle this. He kissed her forehead, prompting her to look those big brown eyes he loved, absolutely adored, up to him. And just by that look in those eyes, he knew she, too, had been wondering down the same road.

Only she hesitated before talking, as if she was unsure if she should go there, but she went there anyway. "I could fall in love with you," she admitted, her hand resting on his flat, ribbed-lined stomach. "You know that, right?"

Dutch continued to rub her hair, continued to look into her eyes. "Yes," he said.

She hesitated again, unsure what to make of his one-word answer. "Do you recommend it?" she asked and waited for his response.

Dutch pulled her closer against him. "It's going to be tough, Regina," he said, and then looked down at her. "And I'm not sure if you understand just how tough." Then he tightened his jaw and stiffened his resolve. He couldn't be selfish with her, not as his feelings for her were beginning to intensify to a point he knew could quickly lead to no return. "I wouldn't recommend it," he said.

Gina's heart dropped, and she lay her head back down on his chest. She understood why he wouldn't recommend it. She understood that he dreaded getting her caught up in that fishbowl life he talked about. But what he didn't understand was that turning back now for her just might not be an option. It would be like un-breaking a heart. She would eventually fall out of love with him, yes, but the damage would have already been done.

She closed her eyes, refused to think about that now. "Why is it called Mirth?" she asked him.

At first Dutch was thrown. *What*, he wanted to say. Then he decided some things, some thoughts, were better left unsaid. He moved on, too. "Mirth means whimsical, happy, cheerful. It doesn't take itself seriously. It's everything Washington is not. That's why it's my favorite restaurant in DC. When I was a lowly bachelor US Senator, I ate many meals there."

"And now you're a lowly bachelor president," Gina said, "and still eating meals there."

Dutch didn't smile the way Gina thought he would. He, instead, closed his eyes too. "Yes," he said, pulling her closer still. "But not for long," he added.

For him to say that, the man who wouldn't even recommend she fall in love with him, confused more than elated Gina. And she decided that he was as terrified of their relationship as she was, and they both therefore needed to just chill.

She closed her eyes, he kept his closed, and they chilled.

Early the next morning, Christian made his way inside the residence to awaken Gina and whisk her away before the press office cranked up. But when he opened the bedroom door, and saw the bed not only empty, but completely undisturbed, he panicked. And hurried to the president's bedroom.

When he opened the door, ever so slowly in case he was still asleep, he was pleasantly surprised to see Gina asleep in the president's arms. And the president held her so protectively, Christian thought, his arms encircling her, her obviously naked body pinned tightly against his. And it was an amazing sight to see. In all of Christian's time in service at the White House, in all the times he had ushered so many different women in and out, he had never arrived to find one of them in the president's own bed. Not ever.

Until now, he thought with a satisfied smile, as he backed back out, and closed the door.

Max Brennan sat on the sofa in the residence and tried his best to get Dutch to listen to reason. But Dutch, who sat in the chair flanking the sofa, had heard it all already.

"But we don't need this fight, Dutch," Max insisted. "Vetoing an appropriations bill when we're trying to get our health care law through is ridiculous. You know how Washington works. It'll be weeks of partisan bickering before we can get anything done."

"That bill was loaded with pork and you know it, and devastating for poor people who rely on social programs. I'll sign it, when they clean that shit up."

Dutch stood to his feet, causing Max to stand, too. "You've got to trust me on this one, Max. If I buckle and allow myself to become like them, then the American people are going to start asking themselves why did they vote for me if I'm no different than the other guy."

Max put both hands in the pockets of his wrinkled suit. "Okay, I trust your political instincts. They've served us well in the past. But. . ." He was looking toward the corridor that led to the bedrooms. Dutch looked too and saw Gina standing there.

"I didn't realize you had company," she said, looking more at Max, who seemed mortified, than Dutch.

"Come on in," Dutch said, glancing at Max too.

Gina was dressed, in an airy summer print dress with matching slip-on sandals, and had one of those big, Fall hats in her hands. She had expected to be taken to a hotel late last night, only to end up in bed with Dutch and awaken to find her luggage in his room. Dutch was casually dressed, in a pair of Khaki pants, a pullover knit shirt, and desert boots, and Gina smiled when he took her by the hand.

"Max, you remember Gina, don't you?"

Max had the look of a man who couldn't believe his bad luck. He stared at Gina. "Gina?" he said.

"Yes," Dutch said. "Regina Lansing. She was one of the recipients of the Mountain Movers award."

"I know what she received," Max said. "And I also know what she dished out. Especially the part about how disappointed she was in your administration. Which begs the question: what the hell is she doing here?"

Dutch and Max grew up together, as their fathers were best friends, and Dutch allowed his friend a lot of liberties with him. But he was coming very close to crossing the line. "She spent the night with me," Dutch said, as if daring his friend to object. "That's what she's doing here."

Max was still astounded by this revelation, but knew not to pursue it. Dutch moved on too, placing his hands on Gina's shoulders and turning her towards him. "I've got some meetings this morning," he said.

"Even on a Saturday?"

"Even on Saturdays, yes. But I should wrap up around two. Christian will be here shortly to take you around, show you the town, all right?"

Gina felt a little flustered, as if she'd ceded control to someone else, and she wasn't sure if she liked it. Dutch saw her apprehension.

"It's all right," he said. Then he reached into his pants pocket, pulled out his wallet, and handed her a credit card. "Here's my card," he said. "Go shopping, go to the spa, pamper yourself a little. Chris will have you back here just in time for me to take you to the Wizards game. You do like basketball, don't you?"

Gina stared at the card and then up at Dutch. "Yes," Gina said, "but. . . "

"But what?"

"This is a credit card with your name on it."

"So?"

"So you're the President of the United States. I can't walk into some store somewhere and expect them to let me use your card. They'll have me under the jail!"

Dutch laughed. "I guess you have a point. Max, give me one of your cards."

"No!" Gina said. No way was she taking any card of his, she wanted to add. "I can pay my own way."

"Sure?"

"Positive."

Dutch nodded. "Okay." Kissed her on her forehead. "I'd better run. See you this afternoon," he said as he began to leave, with Max following behind him. "Chris is on his way," he added, glancing back as he walked. He loved the way that bright, floral print brought out the beauty of her smooth black skin. Just lovely, he thought to himself as he left.

Gina took a seat on the sofa and tried to feel as good as Dutch seemed to think she looked. But she kept feeling as if things were moving too fast for her. In fact, it wasn't until Dutch and Max had left did she realize that she still had his card in her hand.

LaLa, Demps, and Frank sat at their usual table in Cribb's playing cards and drinking beer. It was their usual Saturday afternoon get together and Frank was disappointed to see that one of their foursome, specifically Gina, wasn't there.

"Where is she?" he asked LaLa when he returned from the bar with his glass of beer and sat across from her and Demps.

"There," LaLa said, pointing to the TV nearest them, the TV that was turned to the NBA network telecasting the Wizards game.

Frank looked at the TV. "Where?" he asked. "At that Washington Wizards game?"

"Yup. I called her but she couldn't talk, said she was on her way to the game."

Frank looked disturbed. "I didn't know she was in DC," he said.

LaLa and Dempsey exchanged a glance. "Yeah, she got there Friday night."

"On business?"

"You can say that, yes," LaLa said.

"The President is in the house," one of the three TV commentators said and both LaLa and Dempsey, knowing that Gina had gone to DC on the president's invitation and would most likely be attending the Wizards game with him, immediately looked up at the TV. Frank, completely in the dark, followed their suddenly interested eyes and looked up, too.

"President Harber is in the house," the commentator continued as the camera searched the crowd. "Ah, there he is, making his way to his usual seat on the front row."

And sure enough, LaLa, Dempsey and an astonished Frank looked on as the cameras captured Dutch, his hand on the small of Gina's back, as they were escorted to front row seats.

"Who's that lady with the president?" another one of the commentators wanted to know.

"Pretty lady," the first one commented. "Well-endowed," he joked.

"She's a new one," still the third one said. "'Who's that lady?"

"*Gina*?" Frank said, not in answering their question, but in questioning his own, astounded eyes.

ELEVEN

The door to Max's West Wing office flew open and Allison Shearer, the president's press secretary, hurried in, slammed the door shut, and then walked up to the desk and slung a newspaper onto it. Max, who was on the phone, told the party he'd call them back, and hung up.

"What's this?" he asked. Then picked up the paper.

"You see that headline?" Allison asked. "'Who's that Lady,'" it says. And there's a picture of the president with some . . . person." Allison frowned. "According to that article, she's the woman who told him off at that awards ceremony."

Max was still reading the article. "One in the same." Then he tossed the paper aside. "This is crap. A slow news day. Don't worry about it."

Allison picked up the paper again. "She wore an off the rack, excruciatingly loud print dress, flip flops, and a big flop hat."

"She did not wear flip flops."

"You get their point." Then Allison kept reading. "'She's a big-busted lady with more than her share of curves.'"

Max grinned. "They said that?"

"This can get ugly fast, Max," Allison said. "I fail to see the humor."

The door was opened and yet another aide entered carrying a newspaper. She, too, tossed it onto Max's desk. "Did you guys see this?" she asked.

Allison grabbed it and read the headline aloud.: "'President attends Wizards' game with woman who gave him the finger.'" She put the paper back on Max's desk. "How nice," she said sarcastically. "Such lovely people to write such beautiful words."

"There's more," the aide said. "All over the internet they're joking that the president has found himself a HipHop Queen, and that there's a hood rat in the White House. And then there's another headline: 'The President and his Lady. A Step down from Kate?'"

"It never fails," Allison said. "Every time he dates a new woman they dredge up Kate Marris.

Max's door flew open again and this time Christian entered. "No newspaper," Max asked him. "You're slipping, Chris."

Christian stood before Max's desk, but couldn't seem to want to begin. They all stared at him. "What?" Max asked impatiently.

Christian swallowed hard. "Director Munford's office says he's on his way to see you, sir."

"What about?"

Christian glanced at Allison.

"It's about the lady, isn't it?" Allison asked. "It's about this Regina Lansing?"

"Yes, ma'am," Christian said.

"Well what is it, man?" Max asked. "Spit it out!"

"She's been arrested before," Christian said quickly, and Max, fit to be tied, fell back in his chair.

Dutch's penis slid in and out of Gina with the ease of a man who knew that tunnel so well. He loved the feel and tightness of her, he loved the way she was always so wet and juicy. And his movements quickened when she moaned. He pulled her closer against him as he began to pound her. And just when he released, just when he spilled into her with a push out that caused him a shutter-like spasm, the phone rang.

He collapsed into her arms, his breathing heavy and hard. His phone never rang unless it was urgent.

"We need to meet," Max said.

"Involving?"

"Miss Regina Lansing."

Dutch paused. "I'll be there," he said, and hung up the phone.

He laid back down beside Gina, pulled her into his arms. "Here we go," he said, somehow feeling the onslaught was just beginning.

In the west sitting room of the residence, Max and Allison stood to their feet as Dutch, in a silk red robe, and Gina, in a pair of jeans and a jersey, came into the room. Max glanced at Allison when he realized Gina was with Dutch, but he didn't bother to argue the point. This meeting was, after all, all about her.

"Good morning," Dutch said as he and Gina walked toward the sofa. "Have a seat. Allison, you've met Gina, haven't you?"

"No, sir, I don't think I have," Allison said. "Hello Gina. It is okay for me to call you Gina?"

"Yes, please," Gina said.

"Allison's my press secretary, babe," Dutch said as he and Gina sat on the sofa.

Gina and Allison shared a smile. Everybody in America, if they followed DC politics even a little bit, knew Allison Shearer. She was on cable news, as the president's mouthpiece, almost every day.

"Hope I didn't interrupt anything," Max said, knowing full well, from the breathless way the president answered the phone call, that he had been pounding the mess out of that young lady.

"What's this about?" Dutch asked, a flash of Gina's black body arching up to his white body dancing across his mind. He leaned back and crossed his legs. Gina continued to sit on the edge.

"I had a meeting with Bob Munford this morning," Max said.

"And?"

"And I just want to know how you plan to handle the arrest."

Dutch frowned. "What arrest?"

Max looked at Gina. "What?" she asked Max. When he continued to stare at her, she thought again. And then shook her head. "I don't have a record, I don't know what you're talking about."

"I didn't ask if you had a record," Max said. "I asked if you were ever arrested."

Gina was lost. She had to think hard. When it hit, it still confused her. "But that was nothing," she said and Dutch looked at her.

Allison sighed in frustration. "So it's true?" she asked Gina.

"It was nothing," Gina said again.

"What was it?" Dutch asked.

Gina turned toward him. "I was in college, if that's what they're talking about. And we were protesting one of the professors who gutted many legal aid programs for the poor back when he was a politician, before he became a professor. Things got out of hand--"

"Property was destroyed," Max added.

"And the cops arrested a handful of us, that's true. But the charges were dropped like right away. We cleaned up the little property damage. It was nothing."

Max looked at Allison.

"What is it?" Dutch asked him.

Max leaned forward. "You were protesting with the USJ party, correct?"

"Yes," Gina said, still not understanding why that would be a big deal.

"And what, Gina, does USJ stand for?"

"It was the United Social Justice party, or something like that."

"United Socialists for Justice Party, to be exact," Max corrected her.

"What's the difference? It's a social justice party."

"It's a socialists for social justice party. That's the difference!" Max's anger was rising. Dutch stared at Gina. "Were you a member, Regina?" he asked her.

Gina looked at him. She actually had to think about it. "I certainly attended some meetings. And yeah, I think I was a member."

As soon as she confirmed that she was a member of a socialists group, Max dropped his head in disgust, shaking it. Allison ran her hand through her long, blonde hair and tossed it behind her, murmuring "terrific," as she did. And Dutch, to Gina's dismay, seemed to be riddled with concern.

"What?" Gina asked him. "It was just for a year, I didn't even renew my membership. I know this because it was dues-based and if you didn't pay your dues you were dropped as a member. What's the big deal?"

The look of concern on Dutch's face made her think harder. The USJ party. United Socialists for Social Justice party. Socialists. As in *not capitalists*. As in *un-American*. Gina's heart dropped.

"Oh, Dutch," she said. "But it wasn't about politics for me."

"Then why the hell did you have to join a political group if it wasn't political?" Max asked this angrily and Dutch didn't admonish him. Which meant, to Gina, that he agreed with his chief of staff.

"I joined for that one time because it was a social justice party," she said. "Because they believed in helping their neighbors, in doing all they could for their fellow man. Because I never had any intentions of being a politician and therefore never had to worry about how it would look. Because they believed in social justice!"

"So you're a socialist?" Max asked her.

"No, I'm not a socialist! I was just. . ." She turned to Dutch, to get him to understand. "I wasn't thinking of it as a political party. They helped the poor get good legal help. And I would volunteer to help out. That's why we were protesting that professor. When he was a politician he always would propose bills that would gut all kinds of legal aid for the poor. But that was over fifteen years ago. I was an idealistic kid. I just liked what they stood for at the time." She stared at Dutch. "Your opponents can't use that against you, can they?"

"They can and they will," Max said.

Dutch placed his hand on her shoulder. "We'll handle it."

"Is there anything else we need to know?" Allison asked her.

"What do you mean anything else? I didn't think it was going to be this."

"This is Washington, lady," Max started but Dutch interrupted him.

"Okay, Max, that's enough. You're upset, we're all upset, but you will not talk to her that way, understand me?"

Max nodded. "Understood, sir."

"She doesn't exist inside the beltway," Dutch continued. "Normal people with normal lives doesn't think that what they did fifteen years ago, especially something of so little consequence, would matter now."

"They would think so if they were sleeping with the head of the beltway." Max said this and then seemed to regret it instantly. He exhaled.

"I apologize for that, Miss Lansing."

Gina ignored him.

"Is there anything else you can think of, Gina?" Allison asked her. "Anything else we need to know?"

"Forget whether we need to know it or not," Max said. "Is there any other little nothing incident in your past that we need to be aware of?"

"No."

"Think, Gina," Max said. "The worst thing that can happen is for this story to get legs by drips and drabs."

"It won't gain any traction. There's nothing more to it."

"No other arrests?" Max asked her.

Gina looked at him. "Didn't I say no? No," she said again.

"Don't look at me like that," Max said. "You should have told the president about USJ. Now he's got to clean up your mess."

"He doesn't have to clean up anything of mine," Gina said forcefully. She was getting tired of Max's arrogance. "Now if his opponents want to paint me as some flaming socialist just because I joined a social justice group, then I don't see where reasoning with people like that would matter."

"I agree," Dutch said. Gina looked at him. "It's all right," he said, attempting to smile.

"Dutch, can we--" Max asked, motioning for him to get rid of Gina.

"Yes," Dutch said to Max and then looked at Gina. "Max and Allison and I need to talk. Why don't you go shower and dress so you won't miss your plane."

"I didn't even remember that incident, Dutch, I didn't--"

"I know," he said, rubbing her shoulder. "It's going to be okay. Just don't worry about that now." He leaned forward and kissed her on the lips. Allison looked at Max. Max shook his head.

When Gina left the room, Dutch ran his hand through his hair, tousling it. "Damn," he said.

"Damn is right," Max said, standing and walking around the room. "This is going to be blown all out of proportion, Dutch, and you know it."

"I just don't want her hurt," Dutch said and both of his assistants looked at him.

"Well then you should not have invited her into your life," Max admonished.

"She's certainly different than your usual fare," Allison said. "Maybe the fact that she is different, that she's not some rich belle, might work in our favor."

"Oh, Allison leave it out!" Max yelled, rejecting that notion out of hand. "You know how these people are. They won't show her any mercy, and I mean none! The fact that she isn't some rich belle will probably work against her even more. Remember who critics are. They're the same people who come from the same walk of life she comes from. And because their lives haven't turned out the way they had hoped, they will dump on her, criticize everything about her. They will be terrified that her life just might turn out better than theirs. It's like crabs in a pot, is what it is. They see her trying to crawl out, they'll try their level best to snatch her back in with them."

Allison stared at Dutch. "Your relationship with this one," Allison asked him, "is it serious? Is she Miss Right, or Miss Right Now?"

Dutch exhaled. Hesitated. "Yes, it's serious," he said. *And how*, he wanted to say.

"But why her, Dutch?" Max asked. "You want a black woman, fine, have a black woman, I don't care. The country doesn't care. But let her be a Condi Rice for crying out loud. Not some gotdamn Cleopatra Jones!"

Dutch ran his hand through his hair again, tousling it again.

TWELVE

News of the arrest broke overnight on most of the cable news stations, and Gina, who had a tendency to oversleep whenever she felt stressed, woke up late on Tuesday morning to the sound of knocks on the bedroom door. She nearly fell out of bed reaching for her cell phone and then, realizing that it was actually a door knock and not a phone ring, leaned back down.

"Come in," she said. She had decided to stay at LaLa's house for the night, to avoid any reporters who might be sniffing around hers.

When LaLa walked in, she smiled. "I hate to disturb you, Tore, but I don't think you planned to sleep this late."

Gina ran her hand through her braids. "What time is it?" she asked.

"Nearly ten."

"Dang." Then she looked at LaLa. "Why aren't you at the office?"

"I'm not leaving you here alone to get into idon'tknowwhat."

Gina actually smiled. "Any rumblings on the airwaves?" she asked her.

LaLa took the remote and turned on the small, flat screen TV in the room. From CNN to MSNBC there were comments. From conservatives blaming the president, to progressives blaming Gina. It was all a blame game.

"It's like you robbed a bank fifteen years ago the way they're carrying on."

"Turn it off," Gina said, and LaLa obeyed. Then sat down on the edge of the bed.

"Heard from the president?" LaLa asked.

Gina shook her head. "That protest march didn't even enter my mind once, La. I had forgotten all about it. They make it sound like there was a crime committed and then I was arrested, but it wasn't like that. We were taken down as a group for disturbing the peace in a protest march that got out of hand. And what's crazy the charges were dropped that same day and we were let go. It was nothing."

"You know it, girl, and I know it's nothing. But DC has nothing else to do and to them this is major news. Your life will be an open book." Then LaLa paused. "How did the president take it?"

"Bad. He just seemed so taken aback, you know? Like why didn't I tell him, I don't know. And that Max Brennan."

"He's an asshole, isn't he?"

"It's just that he wasn't so concerned about the arrest as the fact that I was once a card-carrying member of USJ."

A private line cell phone Dutch had given to Gina began to ring. Understanding what that meant, Gina quickly grabbed it.

"It's a mess," LaLa was saying. "New phone?" she asked, looking at the phone.

"So it seems," Gina said and answered the phone. "Hi," she said.

It was Dutch. "How are you this morning?"

"Still reeling," she admitted. "You?"

"I'm okay. But I think you need to come here, let your trusted business partner run the day to day business affairs and you come and stay here as my guest for a while."

"But won't the press go nuts about that, too? They may claim we're shacking up in the White House."

Dutch laughed. "Then just come for the weekend. How's that?"

"That'll work."

"All right good. I have to scram, but I want you to stop worrying, all right? Don't watch the news. Do your work, get it done, and then I'll see you Friday."

"Okay, Dutch. See you Friday."

There was a pause. Then he said goodbye and hung up. Gina held her phone a moment longer, and then shut it off, too.

They sat quietly at the dining room table, upstairs at the White House residence. Gina could already see a change in Dutch, even though he seemed pleased to see her earlier. But now, she could see the strain.

"I never thought a decision I made over fifteen years ago could be so interesting to anyone today." She said this with a smile.

"That's how it works in Washington."

"That's stupid."

"Of course it is," he said, and then looked at her. "But it's politics too."

She didn't like the way he had looked at her, as if he was trying to make some point. "I know it's politics," she said.

"No," Dutch said, "I don't think you do know."

"What's that supposed to mean?"

Dutch sat his fork down on his plate of half-eaten food. "I told you, Regina, that this was a fishbowl."

"I know that."

"I told you they were going to be brutal. But instead of thinking hard and making sure that there are no skeletons in any closets, you behave as if we're talking about grown-ups here. There are no grown-ups in Washington, just a pack of blood-thirsty wolves who'll do whatever it takes to bring my presidency down."

Gina stared at him. "You make it sound like I was concealing that information from you. You make it sound like I knew about it, but just decided not to tell you about it."

Dutch leaned back. "That's not what I mean at all. I know you didn't remember it. Hell, I wouldn't have remembered something like that if I was in your shoes. But this is new to me, Gina."

Gina frowned. "What's new to you?"

"Having the woman I love castigated on national television, night after night, over something so trivial it makes me want to resign right now!" Dutch stood from the table and began to pace the room.

Gina stood too, and went to him. He pulled her into his arms. Then she smiled. Looked up to him. "So I'm the woman you love, hun?" she said.

He smiled. "Somehow I knew that little line would be the main point to you."

Gina laughed. "It's not every day the president confesses his love for a girl."

Dutch's look turned serious, somber. "It's not every day the president falls in love." Dutch rubbed her hair, which was now straight and down her back. "I love you, Regina," he said.

Gina's breath caught. "I love you, too, Walter."

Dutch pinched her behind.

"Ouch!" she said.

"Call me Walter again and that spanking I promised you will soon come to past."

Gina laughed. Pinched him back. He reacted by swaying forward, his penis ramming her. And the sudden contact caused both of them to smile no more. Dutch put his hands on the sides of her face, and began to kiss her so gently, so sweetly, that Gina found herself enraptured.

Back in Newark at BBR, LaLa and Dempsey were going over the monthly receipts when Frank came in asking if they had seen the news.

"Stay away from the news," Dempsey said. "At least until they get off of their Bash Gina kick."

But Frank turned on the office television anyway. There was a press conference in the White House briefing room, with Allison and Max at the lectern.

"She's not his girlfriend," Max was saying and both LaLa and Dempsey looked up at the TV screen.

"But why is he cavorting with a socialist?"

"She's not a socialist," Allison said. "And you know it, Dale."

"The fact remains," another reporter shouted, "that the president's girlfriend was arrested--"

"She's not his girlfriend," Allison insisted.

"Can I finish my question?" the reporter asked.

"No," Allison said. "Not if you're going to distort facts. She's not the president's girlfriend. Let's get that straight. She's a friend. He has many female friends, and she's just one of them. But she's not his girlfriend."

Frank looked at LaLa and Dempsey. "Not his girlfriend," Frank asked, "but his whore?"

Dempsey looked at LaLa. "Frank's right," he said to her. "Not his girlfriend, but she spends every weekend with him now. With *Wham, Bam Harber*, the hit and run specialist. And when he finishes his hit, and he runs, where is that gonna leave Gina?"

LaLa leaned back. Dempsey began to worry more than he already had. And Frank, who sighed outwardly, was inwardly thrilled that that lame president of theirs would be dumping Gina sooner rather than later and pave the way for him to worm his way back into her heart and, eventually, into her bed.

And not one of them, in the BBR office, nor Dutch and Gina at the White House, had any inkling that the worst was yet to come. And this little episode about some socialism party, about some arrest that really wasn't much of an arrest to begin with, would be like a pebble on a beach, like nothingness, compared to what was coming when new news broke, news they had no way of even anticipating, let alone countering with an adequate response.

THIRTEEN

The president slapped the ball across the table expecting Gina to flub it, but Gina was ready. She slapped the ball across, whipping it just as hard as Dutch had, and the game was on. They laughed as they played, their ping pong paddles turning the little-used White House game room into a loud, rip-roaring fun factory for a change. Christian was there too, keeping score, although it was obvious that who won, or who lost, took a far second to enjoying the game.

That enjoyment, however, was short-lived when Dutch got word that Max and Allison needed to see him.

Dutch grabbed a couple towels, threw one to Gina, and began to wipe his face. They were both in shorts, t-shirts and tennis shoes. Had been on the treadmill earlier and had planned to just relax all day. It was Saturday, there was nothing on the president's schedule, and he was determined to enjoy every minute of freedom he had with Gina. And now this.

"Chris you take my place," he told Christian, handing him the paddle. "And don't you cut her any slack."

"Oh, no sir," Christian said with a smile, enjoying the day himself, "she's definitely a gamer."

Gina and Dutch laughed. And although Dutch didn't let on around Gina, he was concerned. His chief of staff and press secretary disturbing him at the residence on a Saturday afternoon automatically meant that something that absolutely couldn't wait was up. And it wasn't any world event that was up, or a cabinet secretary would have phoned him. This, Dutch thought sadly as he made his way to the sitting room, was personal.

Allison and Max stood to their feet when Dutch entered the room. He sat in the chair flanking the sofa. When Dutch was seated, both of them sat back on the sofa.

"Okay, give," Dutch said as he crossed his legs. "Why did the two of you feel a need to disturb me today?"

"It's vital, sir," Max said. "Or you know I wouldn't be here."

"What is it?"

Max looked at Allison. Allison leaned forward. "Sir, did you know that Miss Lansing has a brother?"

"A brother?"

"Yes, sir. A half brother by the name of Marcus Rance?"

Dutch shook his head. "No, she never mentioned such a person."

"They have the same father, sir. Or had since their father is deceased."

"I take it there's a problem with the brother?" he asked.

Max shook his head. "That's the understatement of the century," he said.

Dutch braced himself. "What is it?"

Max was too drained by the news to speak of it. He looked at Allison again.

"The brother, Marcus Rance, is currently in prison, sir."

Dutch's heart tightened. "What for?"

"Murdering a family," Allison said, and Dutch's heart dropped.

"He's on death row, Dutch," Max said.

Dutch leaned back. "Dear God," he said. Then he looked at Max. "What's the story on this guy?"

"Drug dealer. And I mean major. It was a drive-by shooting. Didn't care who he hit, just as long as he hit some punk who happened to be at the house for some Fourth of July celebration. Both parents, three of their five children, and two other partygoers were killed. The punk he was gunning for wasn't even hit."

Dutch shook his head. Thought about what the press would do to Gina with this one. Max moved to the edge of his seat. "Just as we're about to get your reelection campaign cranked up into high gear, this pops up. And once again, she'll claim ignorance. Are you sure she isn't some plant for the opposition, Dutch?"

"Cut that out, you understand me?"

"Yes, sir."

"Cut that the fuck out, do you hear me clearly, Max?"

"Yes. I apologize, sir. But, Dutch, man, this is a problem."

"I know it's a problem. I don't need you to tell me it's a problem."

Dutch picked up the phone on the side table, pressed a button.

"Yes, sir?" Christian said on the other line.

"Bring Miss Lansing to me."

"Yes, sir."

Dutch hung up. When Gina and Christian arrived, they all stood up. Dutch motioned for her to sit next to him.

"Get lost, Chris," Max said to Christian and Christian, after Dutch's nod, left.

"What's the matter now?" Gina asked Dutch. She was still in her shorts and t-shirt, still feeling the effects of a hearty workout. But it didn't take a genius to feel the tension in the room.

"Marcus Rance," Max said and all three of them looked at her.

But Gina frowned. "Who's Marcus Rance?"

"Oh, for crying out loud!" Max yelled. "You expect us to believe that you never heard of your own brother?"

"My brother? I don't have a brother! And don't you yell at me!"

They all stared at Gina. "You didn't know that your father had a son?"

There was a long pause. "I mean, I knew--"

"Oh, great," Max said, and Allison rolled her eyes.

Gina was so tired of these people making her out to be some idiot, when their obsession with the fringes of her life was the real idiocy. She exhaled. "I knew my father had a son out of wedlock, okay, before he married my mother. But he had no contact with that boy, far as I knew, and I didn't even know his name, where he lived, or anything about him. When I was fifteen and my parents died in a car accident, and I asked my aunt if she was going to try and find this boy of my father's, she said my father had one child, me, and that was the end of that. So, that was the end of that."

"Not quite," Max said. "Especially since your father was paying child support for many years to this non-existent brother of yours."

"Child support?" Dutch asked.

"Yes, sir," Max said. "And it's DNA confirmed," Max added.

Dutch stood up and began to walk around the room.

"Have you ever met this man before, this Marcus Rance?" Allison asked Gina.

"Please say never," Max said.

"Never."

"At least there's that," Allison said.

"But, I assure you, Miss Lansing," Max said, visibly agitated, "when the opposition gets a whole of this bit of information they will make it seem as if you and Mr. Marcus Rance are joined at the hip. Siamese Twins, the two of you will be. They will make it seem as though no sister could possibly mean more to a brother, and vice versa, than you and Marcus mean to each other. In other words, they will excoriate you, my dear, when this gets out."

Dutch stood at the lunette window and stared at the activity going in and out of the Old

Executive Office Building. "Will it get out?" Dutch asked, still looking out of the window, his heart pounding, his soul pained at just the thought of the harsh judgments Gina could endure.

"The story will break tomorrow," Allison said. "Somebody in Director Munford's office has leaked it to The Post already. The Post has asked for us to comment prior to going live."

"No comment."

"They want us to say something, sir," Allison insisted, but Dutch interrupted her.

"No comment," he said, turning and looking at Allison. "I don't give a good gotdamn what they want or don't want, I am not legitimizing this nonsense! Regina didn't even know this man existed until we told her, and now they want to act as if she was responsible for his behavior? No. No comment. And I mean hell no."

The exhaustion on Allison's face told her story. Being a press secretary when your boss will not even allow you to speak to the press on a subject that was sure to explode all across the country in twenty-four hours, was a hard pill to swallow.

"What's the story?" Gina asked. "What has this Marcus Rance done?"

Max and Allison looked at Dutch. Dutch walked back over to the sofa, reached out his hand to Gina. When Gina stood, he grasped her. "Marcus Rance is currently on death row for murdering six people."

Gina, stunned, nearly collapsed. But Dutch held her up. With tears in his eyes, he held her up.

Max and Allison left the residence and headed downstairs, to their offices on the West Wing. They walked as if they were in a funeral procession. When they arrived at Max's office, Max went behind his desk, picked up his telephone, and dialed a once very familiar number.

"We're dead, you know that?" Allison said.

"I know."

"Who are you calling?"

"Kate Marris."

Allison stared at Max. "The president's ex? Are you sure?"

"What the hell else can we do? You saw him? He doesn't even want us to comment. He's running for reelection, will be in the fight of his life, and he decides to date some sister-girl from the hood with more baggage than Samsonite! You'd better believe I'm sure."

Then a familiar voice came onto the line. "Kate, darling, how are you?" Max said into the phone. "It's Max Brennan. No, it's not a social call. This call is strictly business." Then Max exhaled, looked at Allison. "He needs you, Kate," he said.

FOURTEEN

Two weeks later and the story was still a big topic of conversation. Although there had been a few disasters, like more flooding along the southern plain states, nothing so severe that it would knock Marcus Rance and his shady life off of the front pages.

The staff at BBR, however, were no longer bombarded with reporters camped outside their office doors, or at their homes, but the effects of the last two weeks were being felt in their donations. Down mightily, by all accounts.

They sat at the conference table, Gina, LaLa, Demps, and Frank, and tried to make sense of it all. But they couldn't. It was nonsensical.

Gina stared at a picture of her half-brother, and she could see no resemblance to her father at all. The caption read: The President's Brother-in-law?

"They know I have never had anything to do with this guy," she said. "Every reporter in

America knows that I don't even know him. But they continue to print this craziness! And now it's hurting BBR."

"Even our local paper," Frank said, "hasn't been immune. They claimed that's the real reason why you started BBR. Because you saw the waywardness of your brother."

Gina shook her head. It was too much. And this story, unlike the faux arrest story, couldn't' be ignored.

That was why they spent most of the morning watching news accounts, amazed at how, not just Dutch's political opponents, but reporters as well were linking her to Marcus Rance. Now the president was speaking at the White House about a meeting he had just wrapped up with the prime minister of Pakistan, who stood beside him in the Rose Garden, and the very first question by reporters wasn't about the US-Pakistani relationship, or the war in Afghanistan. It was about Marcus Rance.

"I don't condone murder, first of all," Dutch had to clarify based upon the reporter's question, and it was downhill from there. Yes, they had the same father, but no, she never met him, didn't have any relationship, didn't know he existed until the story broke. But the very next question would be, once again, about this unknown half-brother of Regina Lansing's and why it wasn't made public sooner.

Gina, for her part, could only stare at the screen. "It's bad, isn't it?" she asked Dempsey. "For the president, I mean?"

Dempsey glanced at LaLa, who was horrified by it all. Dempsey leaned forward. "When the President of the United States has to begin an answer by saying he doesn't condone murder, as if it's implied that he might, yeah, it's bad."

Gina frowned. "It's so unfair," she said.

"Politics and fairness are nonexistent bedfellows," Frank said, and LaLa looked at him.

At the Mirth restaurant and Dutch and Max were eating alone. It was Max's idea. Get out of the White House, show the press that you're moving on. Dutch knew it was also to show the press that Gina wasn't in town, but he was hungry and lonely, so he agreed.

They were a few minutes into their meal and conversation when the door was opened within the private room and Katherine Marris, blonde, blue-eyed, and voluptuous, walked in.

When Dutch saw her, he sat his fork on his plate. Max stood to his feet.

"Hello, Darling," Kate said to Max, air-kissing him on both cheeks.

"How are you, Kate?"

"Famished," she said, sitting down in Max's seat and removing her gloves. "A gentleman," she said to Dutch, "would have stood for a lady."

"If I had seen a lady," replied Dutch, "I would have stood."

"Ouch," Max said with a smile.

"What is she doing here?" Dutch asked Max. "And who gave her clearance to interrupt my dinner?"

"I did," Max said. He put his hands in his pockets, revealing a belly flapped over his belt. "I asked her to talk to you."

Dutch stared at Max. He just didn't get it. He thought Gina was just a temp, just like all of his previous ladies, and Kate was the true love of his life. She wasn't, and never was, but Max didn't believe it.

When Max had excused himself from the room, Dutch leaned back and folded his arms. "All right," he said. "You're here to talk, then talk."

Kate smiled, picked up a carrot off of Max's plate and took a bite. "You haven't changed at all," she said. "But I love you, too." Then she sighed. "It was Max's idea, darling, believe that. He's under the impression that I still have some sort of influence over you, foolish man." She looked at Dutch. "He's worried about you."

Their eyes met. In Dutch, Kate did see the love of her life, a man she still found herself crying over. In Kate, Dutch saw the woman who had given him an ultimatum. Marry her, she'd said, or leave her. He wasn't about to marry her, there was too much character lacking in hers, and he called it quits.

"And besides," Kate said, "I've missed you."

Dutch could have strangled Max if he was still in the room. The last thing he wanted to do right now was get into it with Kate. He began eating his dinner again. "I saw you at that fundraiser last month with that actor, what's his name? I'm glad to see you've moved right along."

"Well, what did you want me to do? Cry in a corner over you?"

"Of course not," Dutch said with a look of alarm on his face. "I don't want you to do anything over me. It's over between us. Completely over."

A sadness came over Kate's eyes, but she maintained her bravado. "So I'm still out, and the murderer's sister is in?"

"Cute, Kate."

"Thank-you."

"I would not have expected anything less."

Kate felt the verbal jab, but ducked. "That woman, and this is what they're saying in our circles, could cost you your reelection bid. You know that, right?"

"People say a lot of things."

"But *her*, Dutch, come on. She's everything we aren't. It's as if you're trying to prove some point. And it's a ridiculous point."

Dutch continued to eat. And Kate continued to talk. And at the end of the evening, they headed out by the side exit, with Dutch more than ready to go his way, and Kate supposedly going hers.

But the press was out in force, with cameras flashing as soon as they exited the building. Kate immediately placed her arm within his and then stumbled against him, causing him to react by catching her. The flashbulbs went crazy. Dutch removed her from his grasp, and hurried for his limousine.

Less than two hours later, Frank was at Gina's front door. "Thought I'd come over in case you needed a shoulder to cry on," he said as she reluctantly let him into her home. But this time it was his statement, rather than that odd feeling she got whenever he was around her, that concerned her.

"Cry? Why would I need a shoulder to cry on?"

Frank stopped in his tracks. "You mean you haven't seen it?"

"Seen what?"

"The two of them."

Gina frowned. "The two of whom? Frank, what are you talking about?"

Frank walked over to the sofa, put his briefcase up on the table, and pulled out a small portable DVD. "They were showing it so often that I recorded it. Now I'm glad I did. Come here."

Gina walked over to the sofa and sat down. And there it was, Dutch and Kate coming out of Mirth, arm in arm, and then the stumble and then the capture. Kate in the arms of the president, looking like the perfect couple.

"Is that Kate Marris?"

Frank nodded. "That's her. She's supposedly the love of his life." When he said this and looked at Gina, he could see all fight go out of her. Frank, thrilled, kept playing it over and over until Gina stood up quickly and moved away.

"Would you like something to drink, Frank?" she asked him.

"No, I'm good," he said. "It's you I'm worried about. Would *you* like something to drink?"

Gina sat down in the chair, and nodded. "Yes, please," she said.

Frank gave a shy smile and hurried for the kitchen. When he returned, he stood there staring at her. She looked lost, it seemed to him.

"Ah, you poor thing," he said, sitting the glass on the table and hurrying to her. He sat on the edge of the chair and pulled her slightly to him.

"No, I'm okay," she said, resisting his pull.

"But you must be devastated," Frank said, continuing to pull on her.

"Why would I be devastated? He was just having dinner with an old acquainted. That's no big deal."

"That's not what the cable news commentators are saying. They said they looked happy together, like they belonged together." He slammed her against him. "Like us," he said, and put his lips to hers.

Gina was mortified when she realized Frank was kissing her. She jerked away from him and then slapped him hard across the face. "What do you think you're doing?" she asked him, astounded.

But Frank was not to be denied. "You know what I'm doing, bitch," he said, grabbing her again, "and you know you like it!"

He began kissing her again. This time Gina's strength was no match for his and she was unable to break free. She, instead, kneed him in the groin. He turned her loose then, bent down to absorb the pain, and then looked back up at her.

"Get the hell out of my house and get out now!" she demanded.

"You bitch!" Frank shouted and took his fist and hit her, as hard as he could, across the face. And he didn't stop. He couldn't stop. He pounded her, as if he was pounding on a punching bag, blood spewing from her, beating her until she was on the floor, begging for mercy.

Gina tried to fight back, she kept swinging at him and screaming and doing everything she could to stave him off. But he was too powerful. And too out of his mind with that maniac's strength. And then the little strength she did have was gone. He hit her one more time, and she was down and out and unmovable.

Frank at first felt triumphant. He just taught that bitch something. He even ripped off all of her clothes and pulled out his penis ready to ram it in and get what he'd been wanting since the day he first saw that beautiful black body walk into his office and asked if his company would support BBR. But then he realized, seeing her lifeless body, seeing the blood, what he had just done. He backed up, falling down to his knees, and began to cry. What had he done? He never meant for this to get so out of control!

He began to run, but realized again that the evidence, his briefcase, his portable DVD, were still sitting on her coffee table. He ran back, grabbed both, and stopped at the foot of Gina's naked body. He fell to his knees again. Tears were once again in his eyes.

"You should have loved me," he said. "None of this would have ever happened, if you would have loved me!"

Then he stiffened his resolve. Stood up and stood taller. Zipped up his pants. "Got exactly what you deserved, bitch," he said defiantly, angrily. But then he started to cry again, and then moved right, then left, and then dropped his briefcase and DVD and fell down. He took her in his arms, hugging her body to his, crying *oh, Gina*, over and over. And then he slung her away from him, his mind reminding him that he wasn't holding Gina, but was holding a dead woman, a woman killed by his own hands, and he grabbed his briefcase, his portable DVD once again, and hurried out of her front door.

The phone kept ringing and Dutch hung up. It was his third try to reach her in the past hour. He was seated on the edge of his bed, in his robe and slippers, amazed that reputable cable news channels wouldn't see through Kate's act and dismiss it. Instead, they were calling it breaking news, showing that little Academy Award caliber performance by Kate at the restaurant, and was running it in loops over and over. He could only imagine what Gina could be thinking.

He phoned her once again. This time, however, he didn't hang up when the voice mail picked up.

"Regina, answer your phone," he ordered. But there was no pick up. He hung up again, certain that she had seen the same footage he was viewing and was purposely avoiding his phone calls.

He'd already warned Max that if this nonsense caused Gina to leave him, he would live to regret ever picking up any phone and calling that vamp

Kate Marris. And within seconds, he was picking up his own phone, and calling Gina yet again.

This time, however, there was an answer.

"Gina?" he said.

"No, sir, it's Dempsey. Dempsey Slater, sir, Gina's friend and business partner."

Dutch frowned. "Where's Regina?"

There was a sigh. "We just found her, sir."

"Found her? What do you mean you just found her?"

"She was. . . She's in bad shape, sir, real bad shape. Lord have mercy! I've never seen so much blood."

"Blood?" Dutch said, standing to his feet, his heart beginning to pound.

"We just got here. We just . . . She wouldn't answer her phone and . .. we, me and LaLa, that's her best friend, came over. She's been rushed to the hospital, sir."

Dutch's heart stopped. "How bad is it?" he managed to asked, resuscitating himself.

"Sir," Dempsey said, "it's bad. It's real bad."

+++

The hospital doors flew open and Dutch entered in a hurry. Secret Service agents fanned out, and

213

a team of doctors stood on the ready for the president, including Dr. Cyril Clyburn, one of the foremost surgeons in the country and a Manhattan physician who was able to get there as quickly as the call came out. He was handpicked by Dutch's people when Dutch insisted that the best they could find consult on the case.

"How is she?" Dutch asked, without breaking his stride, and Cyril and his team hurried to keep up with him.

"She's out of surgery," Cyril said.

Dutch looked at him. "Any complications?"

"None."

"Thank God Almighty!" Dutch said, relieved.

"All of her signs are stable," the doctor went on, "she's responding well to commands. We expect a full recovery, sir."

Dutch thanked God for that, too. He had wanted to get there sooner, but preparing to fly the president on a moment's notice, without there being any national security emergency, wasn't as simple as it would seem. "Is she awake?" he asked the doctor.

"Yes, sir, she's awake. But in and out, of course."

"Understood," Dutch said.

When Dutch arrived at her hospital room, he paused, exhaled, and then went inside.

Gina was lying in bed, going in and out of sleep, when the door of her room opened and Dutch appeared before her. Although her face was heavily bandaged, and she felt like hell, she was beyond glad to see him.

Dutch knew it too because her eyes lit up as if she, too, had just seen the most wonderful sight she could have ever hoped to see again. And he hurried to her, and gently, but definitely, held her in his arms.

He, in fact, would spend that entire night at Gina's bedside, sitting in a chair holding her hand, watching her fade in and out of consciousness, praying continually for her full recovery. And when he did return to Washington, he left Christian at her bedside, and his own personal physician at the ready, to ensure that she had everything she needed, and he meant everything, at her fingertips.

FIFTEEN

The SUV was a part of a convoy of identical vehicles, with two of them there to obfuscate and redirect in case some crack journalist had gotten wind of the fact that the president's girlfriend was no longer at the hospital. The purpose was to transport Gina from Newark to be near Dutch in DC.

The SUV drove onto the driveway of a Tudor-style Georgetown home, around a long curve, to the garage in the back. Once inside the garage, and the garage door down, Gina could see more security in the garage, talking into their wristbands. And she sighed. It all seemed so elaborate, so unnecessary to her. But what could she do? She wanted to be with Dutch, Dutch wanted her with him, something had to give.

"We're home," LaLa said jokingly as they stepped out of the SUV. In addition to Christian, who remained in Newark during Gina's entire week of recovery, LaLa and Dempsey were also with her, on Dutch's insistence, and the running of BBR was left to a professional staff of Dutch Harber's business allies.

And when she found out that these business allies included major CEOs, etc, even she had to admit that BBR was probably in better hands with them than it had ever been with her. That appropriations bill was dead, and a new bill was being reworked by Congress, but even with the stall BBR was getting back on sound footing. Donations were pouring in now that major hitters were offering their helping hand.

But that still didn't stop her from finding this all too taxing. "I still don't see why I can't recover at my own home," she said as she and her friends entered the home through the side door. "And to insist that the two of you babysit me is ridiculous."

"We're glad to be here," Dempsey said, "so stop whining."

Gina smiled. He and LaLa were good friends indeed. But just thinking about Frank, and what he did to her, made her blood boil.

They entered the home through the side door, walking down a corridor and then into the living room. When they entered the living room and saw Dutch standing there, LaLa and Dempsey smiled. Chrisitan moved past them to stand by the president's side, happy to see the man he loved almost as much as Gina did.

And Gina, however, just stood there and considered him. He wore a Red Sox baseball cap with jeans and a light green polo shirt, and what struck her was how that didn't seem like much of a disguise at all, if that was his point. But her heart began to pound at the sight of him, and she had to sit down, in the first chair she came to, before she fell.

Dutch hurried to her side. "Are you all right?" he asked. There were still tenderness to her face, but the bruising was down and almost completely gone.

"Yes, I'm fine," she said, smiling. "I'm just glad to see you."

219

Dutch touched her on the nose. And then he stood and looked at Christian.

"Let me show you folks where your rooms will be," Christian said as if on cue, and LaLa and Dempsey, understanding too, hurried behind him.

When they were gone, Dutch stood Gina up, sat down, and put her on his lap. "I've missed you terribly," he said, kissing her on the lips.

"Are you okay?" Gina asked him, seeing the tiredness in his eyes.

"I am now," Dutch said, rubbing her arm. It had been nearly two weeks since Frank's brutal act and he'd only just had a chance to touch her like this. "I wish I didn't have to get back."

"You have to leave?"

"Unfortunately, yes. Meetings and more meetings. But I'll get over here as often as I can. No-one knows you're here, no press. And my security people will continue to see to that. That way I can slip away and come see you, although it'll usually have to be when the press is fast asleep."

"Just when they were playing up that Marcus Rance nonsense, I get into more trouble."

"You didn't get into anything," Dutch reassured her. "You didn't do this to yourself, that asshole did this to you."

"How's the press playing it?" Gina asked. "I refused to watch any coverage."

"The official story is that you had a tumble in your home. The mainstream media is running with that story. The tabloids, however, are claiming you were badly beaten by a jealous boyfriend."

"Oh, great," Gina said. Then she looked at Dutch. "But if the official story is that I fell, then does that mean Frank will get away with what he did to me?"

"That bastard isn't getting away with anything," Dutch said heartfelt. "I assure you of that."

In Cleveland, Ohio, as the night turned into morning, a car swerved into an alley, dumped Frank Roselli from out of its backseat, and sped off. Frank got on his knees, his face so bloody, so swollen, that both of his eyes were swollen shut. He tried to stand up, but fell back down. Crawled some more through the smut and grim of a back alley, and then passed on out.

Nearly a month after the attack, Dutch arrived at Gina's Georgetown residence in the dark of night, three am, after a long dinner party for a Saudi prince. He got naked, tossing his clothes on the back of the chair as if he lived there, crawled into bed, and lay behind her. Gina didn't know he was in bed with her until she felt his naked body against hers, and his warm arms encircle her.

"Oh, Montel, be quick before Dutch gets here," she whispered with a smile.

Dutch slapped her so hard on her naked butt that she nearly slid out of the bed, laughing all the way.

"I've got your *Montel*," Dutch said as he began kissing her neck. She tried to turn around to face him, but he began sucking the first breast that came into his view, stifling her. The thing Gina knew about Dutch was that he always touched her where she ached, so she never tried to steer him or suggest he move in any direction when he made love to her. He always moved in the exact direction she needed him to move into, and tonight was no exception.

She lifted her head, revealing that long, beautiful neck he loved so well. He moved from her breast to her neck, his mouth searing her with every kiss.

He moved her on top of him, and entered her, sucking her beasts as he fucked her, squeezing her ass as she bucked him. Her breasts, taunt and full, were flapping as she rode him. And when she came, it felt as if she was being filled up with warm, sweet liquid that poured into her. She tightened, laid down on top of him in a feeling too intense for her to bear, as his penis penetrated her to the very edge of his balls.

The next day, Dutch had made up his mind. He was in the Oval Office and Max and Allison sat in front of his desk. And although he thought it was a good idea, they thought it was madness.

"We're finally turning a corner," Max said. "Marcus Rance is no longer on front pages, Regina's past arrest or whatever it was is barely mentioned. We're now focused on what we should be focused on, and that's getting you reelected. But for you to erase all of that progress with one false move, and it will be a bad move, is a bridge too far, Dutch."

"Let her be a guest at the state dinner," Allison said. "Let someone be her escort even. But don't join her to you. Not now. This event is too high profile for that. All those old stories will start right back up again."

Dutch heard their arguments. He leaned back in his chair and heard them repeatedly. But they could save their breath. Last night, when he was making love to Gina, when his penis was entering her in a slow, gradual draw-in, he realized the depths of his love. There was no other woman on the face of this earth that he would rather be with. No other woman. And he was tired of hiding her from the world. Say what they want, protest all they pleased, but come tomorrow night, when the Prime Minister of Great Britain got out of that limousine at the White House, Gina was going to be standing right beside him.

And that was exactly what happened. At a state dinner in honor of British Prime Minister David Bellamy and his wife Rebecca Bellamy, the limo drove up and stopped at the North Portico of the White House. Standing on the portico to greet the British couple were President Walter Harber and Regina Lansing, the president's girlfriend. It was official now. No parsing of words, no *she's just a friend like so many other of his female friends*. She was the bona fide girlfriend of the President of the United States. Press rooms and news rooms all across America went haywire.

It wasn't a news room, but a bedroom. And Kate Marris was lying in the bed, her latest boy toy lying beside her. And as soon as the reporter announced that the state dinner was hosted by President Harber and his girlfriend, Regina Lansing, she took the remote control she had in her hand, and tossed it through the television screen, shattering its glass.

At that same time in Cleveland, Ohio, in a nursing home, Frank Rotelli was watching the news reports up front in the TV room. He was blind and wheelchair bound, but was listening to every word.

"What's happening now?" he asked aloud.

"Who cares?" somebody else yelled back, and then they changed the channel. Frank slammed his fist down on the arm of his chair, slammed it until an aide had to be called and wheeled him back to his room. It was nothing unusual. They were accustomed to his outbursts.

Two days later, on a typical work night, Max arrived at the Oval Office with Kate Marris in tow. Dutch, who had been reviewing additional national security risk assessment reports, was about to kick them both out, when Max spoke up.

"You have to hear what she has to say, Dutch," he said.

Dutch could hardly believe it. Max had nearly lost his job behind his other Kate Marris stunt. Now he was at it again? "It better not be any bullshit like that night at Mirth," Dutch warned him.

"This is no bullshit," Max said, looking flustered. "I wish it was, but it's not."

This caught Dutch's attention. And that look in Max's eyes concerned him. "What is it?"

"May I sit down?" Kate asked, hurt that he would treat her so insensitively. She used to rock his world, now he behaved as if she never meant anything to him.

Dutch stood slightly and motioned for her to sit down. He always hated it when girls like Kate, who made no secret of dating guys only for their looks and power, wanted to be taken seriously. "What is it this time?" he asked as soon as they were seated. Max continued to stand. He, in fact, began to pace the circular room.

Kate removed her gloves. Why she was always wearing those gloves, Dutch thought, was beyond him. "I won't beat around the bush," she said. "I know you have more important things to do."

"You're beating around the bush," Dutch said. "Get to the point."

"I'm pregnant with your child and if you don't marry me I'll go to the press with this golden information." Then she stared at him. "Is that pointed enough for you?"

Dutch sat stunned. "Pregnant?"

"Yes." She opened her purse, pulled out a medical statement from her doctor. "Care to see the proof?"

"How do we know it's his?" Max asked her, although he asked it with little reassurance.

"It's his," Kate said. "Before we broke up, he was the only man I was sleeping with."

Max grabbed the medical statement and perused it. "You had gone your separate ways before this," he said, although he knew that wasn't true.

"We went our separate ways, yes, but not before I became pregnant," Kate said. "We broke up just before he latched onto the murderer's sister."

Dutch continued to sit there. Kate and Max both waited for a response. For Max, it was a two-edged sword. On the one hand, if Dutch married Kate that could immediately put an end to their Regina Lansing baggage problem. But on the other hand, eliminating Regina Lansing could alienate their base, especially African-Americans and progressive whites.

But Dutch just sat there, taking his own counsel. Then he seemed to come to some decision. "Is there anything else?" he asked Kate.

Kate glanced at Max. Then stared at Dutch. "No."

"Then you're excused," Dutch said.

"Now wait a minute," Max said but Kate cut him off.

"You think I'm lying?" she asked as she stood up, flapping her gloves together. "You think I won't go to the media if you don't marry me? Well, watch me, dammit. Just watch me, Dutch!"

"Kate, just," Max said, hurrying to her side. "Just give us some time, all right? You just sprang this on us, for crying out loud! At least give us a few days."

"You have two days," she said, putting back on her dainty gloves. "If I don't hear an affirmative in two days, I will go public. I promise you I will. And don't even try that *she's a slut, it's not my baby* Maury Povich shit. You know and I know, too, Dutch, that I was sleeping with you and you alone. Nobody gets fucked by you and then get in bed with some other man. That's an impossibility." She looked at

Dutch, remembering what it was like in bed with him, regretting losing that kind of love, and turned to leave.

When she was gone, Max looked at the president. "If she goes to the media, Dutch," he said, "this story will make Marcus Rance look like Little Red Riding Hood."

Dutch leaned back, suddenly constricted with fear.

SIXTEEN

It felt like a nail in his own coffin. What was supposed to be his triumph after introducing Gina on the world stage, at a state dinner no less, without a glitch, was turning into a funeral march. His own. Meeting after meeting was all about Kate. It had been about the Regina arrest problem. Then the Marcus Rance problem. Now the Kate Marris problem.   And her problem wasn't external to the president. Her problem was the president's problem.

But Dutch wasn't thinking about his problem, or the press, or even his reelection campaign. All he could think about was Gina. All that day and when she arrived at the White House that night to have dinner with him, Gina was on his mind. Yet, it wasn't until after dinner, when they were settled in the sitting room, seated side by side on the sofa, did he find a way to tell her.

She stared at Dutch. "She's *pregnant*?" she asked, astounded.

Dutch took her hand in his, and nodded his head. "I'm afraid so, honey."

"But it's not yours, right? She's not pregnant with your child. Is she?"

Dutch looked into her eyes. "Yes. It's more than likely mine."

Gina couldn't believe it. "But you said you broke up with her, that y'all weren't together anymore."

"We weren't. We aren't. But we've confirmed her medical info. We were still fooling around when she became pregnant."

Tears began to puddle within Gina's eyes, but she held on. "So what's the game plan?" she asked. "What does Max say you have to do?"

"Kate is saying she'll go to the press," Dutch said, looking away from Gina, "unless I marry her."

Gina's eyes stretched. "*Marry her*?"

Dutch nodded. "Yes, sweetie, that's what she's demanding."

"But," Gina said, unable to wrap her brain around such a demand. She looked at

Dutch. "What are you going to do?" she asked
him. "If she goes to the press and says you
impregnated her but won't marry her, that will
ruin you. You aren't that kind of man. But your
political enemies will twist it around and make it
seem as if you've always been some kind of
deadbeat."

"I know," he said. He hated the fact that she
sounded as if she was panicking. She, in fact,
sounded how he felt. But there was no way
around it. This was shocking, devastating news.

"So what are you going to do?" Gina asked
him again, her earnest eyes staring at him as if
expecting him to be his honorable self and say he
had no choice, he had to dump her and wed Kate
Marris.

Dutch, however, got off of the sofa and down
on his knees, his hand still holding Gina's. Gina
stared at him. "Regina Lansing," he said, his eyes
wide with tension, "will you marry me,
sweetheart?"

Gina fell into his arms. There was no thinking
about it, no trying to figure out how in the world
were they going to get around their Kate Marris

problem, there was just love. Her love for him and his love for her.

"Well?" he asked her, tears in his eyes.

"Yes," she said, without hesitation. "Oh, yes!"

Dutch's heart soared. He stood to his feet and lifted her into his arms. It was a wellspring of relief for Dutch, a feeling that Kate and Max and Allison and anybody else who tried to tear them apart, could go to hell.

Thirty miles off of the southern coast of Cape Cod, the presidential helicopter arrived on Nantucket Island amid tight security and privacy, and deposited Dutch and Gina in what was the backyard of the Harber family compound.

Dutch held onto Gina as if she was a fragile doll and they hurried, ducking copter wings, their hair and suits blowing from its wind shear, onto the back colonnade that led into the mansion.

Although Gina had been schooled by Dutch on what to expect, she still felt unprepared. And as they walked down the long porch that looked like a corridor in a roman coliseum, following the butler, she had a sinking feeling that this wasn't going to turn out well. The Harber family consisted of only two people now, Dutch and his mother, Victoria Harber, and nobody was going to tell Gina that that woman, with all of her wealth and position, was not going to have near-impossible expectations for her only son and heir, the President of the United States.

But Dutch was hopeful, although cautiously so. To know his mother is to love her, he had said last night when they laid in bed talking about this very trip. Although they weren't particularly close, Dutch was always more of a father's son than a mama's boy, there was a respect he held for his mother that seemed to Gina to border on the mythical. Which usually meant, she felt, that he probably didn't know his mother's true character much at all.

She marched with Dr. King in the sixties, he said. She was always a liberal voice of reason in Massachusetts politics, he said. She was and remain a defender of the poor and downtrodden, just like you, Gina, he also noted.

But Gina also knew that she was rich, and it had been her experience, when soliciting donations for BBR, that rich liberals were no different than rich conservatives when it came to their family legacy. And no matter how much Gina wanted it, or how grand Dutch talked up his mother's outward attributes, she just couldn't see a woman like Victoria Harber welcoming with open arms a woman like her.

And she was right. Dutch and Gina were shown to the morning room by the butler, where they sat side by side on the sofa and waited for the great dame to arrive. And when she walked in, surprisingly more petite and frail from the photos Gina had seen of her, a coldness came with her that could chill the sun.

Dutch stood and hurried to his mother, kissing her on either cheek. Gina stood and waited, her heart pounding, her worst fears confirmed as soon as the widow Harber turned and looked at her.

"Mother," Dutch said, escorting her toward the couch, "this is Regina Lansing."

"How do you do?" Gina asked with a very slight bow of her head.

"Do you care, or is that what they told you to say to me?"

Gina stared into this woman's hard blue eyes and realized immediately that sugar coating her wasn't going to work. Okay, she thought, so you want to play it that way? "I care because I care about your son," she said. "And yes, they did tell me to say that."

Victoria seemed taken aback, as if she hadn't expected that level of honesty, but it didn't thaw the chill. "Have a seat," she said to Gina.

Gina sat back down while Dutch helped his mother to a flanking chair. They were surrounded by beauty, a home more fancily decorated than the White House, but somehow Gina felt as if beautiful was the last thing in the world this home was about.

When Dutch took his place back beside Gina, taking once again her hand in his, Gina could see his mother's jaw tighten. She expected to have to entertain a tough audience, but nothing like this.

"Since you never come just to say hello to me," Victoria said to her son, a note of bitterness in her often frail voice, "I assume this rare visit has everything to do with this young lady before us."

"That's correct," Dutch said pointblank.

"I see. I saw her at the state dinner, looking marvelous I might add, and my telephone became a hotwire. What is she really like, Vicky, they kept asking me. What's her family like? And I had to say without hesitation that I have no idea. Never met the woman. Had no clue that my son, my only son and heir, had suddenly contracted jungle fever and was now sleeping with the natives."

Gina looked at Dutch. She already had expected venom. But Dutch hadn't. And by that look of disappointment in his eyes, he hadn't expected any venom at all. "Is that how you see my relationship with Regina?" he asked her, studying her.

"How else am I supposed to see it?" Victoria wanted to know. "You haven't exactly given me any beforehand notice. You haven't telephoned or written or even emailed any such information about your relationship. I thought Kate Marris was the love of your life, now here she comes."

Dutch stared at his mother. Where did they get this love of his life nonsense? Was it because Kate was beautiful and blonde and from the kind of family presidents usually married into? It certainly wasn't because of the reality of the relationship, or anything Dutch had said or may have even implied.

But there it was again. Kate was supposed to have been the love of his life, the woman they all had expected him to marry. When, in truth, she was a woman he had never loved, and, other than fucking her, barely liked.

"Kate Marris is not now," he said, "nor ever has been the love of any life of mine."

"Well, you certainly could have fooled me," Victoria said, "the way the two of you were carrying on."

Dutch refused to make this visit about Kate. "Regina has my heart," he told his mother, "and she's the only woman to capture it after Caroline's death. The only woman. And that's why, Mother, I am going to marry her."

Gina looked at Mrs. Harber. The disdain just poured from her. "*Marry her*? Have you taken leave of your senses? Marry *her*? Some poor black from *Newark*? You must be out of your mind! Marry *her*?"

Gina wondered if the woman was going to have a conniption. She was tossing fiery darts

and hitting bull's-eyes as far as Victoria chose to
see it. She was tossing fiery darts and hitting
herself, as far as Gina saw it. Because Dutch just
stared at his mother, his legs crossed, his eyes
filled with a sad disappointment, a shame even,
and, to Gina's surprise, a kind of dislike she had
only seen in Dutch when he spoke of his political
enemies. Now he knew what Gina had known all
along: that rich liberals fighting for liberal causes
in the abstract were well and good, as long as
you didn't bring any of those "causes" to their
front door.

When it was clear that Dutch was not going to
respond to Victoria's verbal attacks, she
exhaled. "What about Kate?" she asked him.

"To hell with Kate!" he yelled back.

"Okay, forget Kate," his mother said. "What
about your child Kate's carrying?"

Dutch was stunned. He had no idea that his
mother even knew about that. "She told you
about that?"

"Of course she did. She's a wonderful girl
who would have made you a wonderful wife, this
country a wonderful First Lady, but you couldn't
see it. Now she's about to have your child, my

first and only grandchild, and you choose to dump her for some . . . some social worker!"

"She's an attorney," Dutch reminded his mother, as is she didn't already know, "not a social worker. And even if she was a social worker, so what? You as well as I know that Kate and I broke up before I began any relationship whatsoever with Regina." *That night in Miami a decade ago notwithstanding*, both he and Gina thought inwardly. "So don't you dare attempt to put any home-wrecker labels on her."

Victoria was surprised by her son's harsh tone. "If your father was alive," she began, but Dutch didn't want to hear it.

"I am going to marry Regina," he said. "That's why I came here. To let you know."

"But what about the child Kate's carrying?"

"If after she delivers and DNA testing proves that I'm the father, I will take care of my child. But I will not marry Kate, a woman I could barely stomach, just for that sake."

"Oh, you can barely stomach her now," Victoria said. "When you were impregnating her just four months ago, you could more than stomach her then. You were loving her then."

"No, mother," Dutch admitted, "I was not loving Kate when I impregnated her. I was just fucking her."

This astounded Victoria. The vulgarity! Even Gina was surprised. And Victoria stood to her feet. Dutch, nor Gina, bothered to move.

"You disgust me," Victoria said with the venom now toxic on her tongue. "You have always disgusted me. That's why our relationship has never been anything but eye candy, a smile, a kiss, hello and goodbye. Because I knew you were like this. I saw it in you as a child. Always had to do things your way, not the way of our circle, but your way. Tried to befriend that little black boy from Cape Cod when you were a child. Always dating black women in college."

"I dated all kinds of women, Mother," Dutch said.

"But you favored the black ones, don't tell me you didn't. Even Caroline, God rest her soul, was said to have some black blood in her. That was your attraction to her, I've always believed. But when you met Kate, I thought that there was hope for you yet. Maybe political reality woke you up to how foolish you'd been and now you were ready to commit to a real woman, a woman with background and breeding, of a pedigree that impressed even me. But oh no, not Dutch. He has to be his own man, do things his own way, love whomever he chooses to love, even if that choice would destroy everything he has worked so hard to build."

She exhaled, looked him dead in the eye. "Well I tell you, Walter Harber, that I will oppose this farce of a marriage with every breath in my body! And I will let the world know how vehemently I oppose it!"

She said this, and just stood there. As if, to Gina's amazement, she expected Dutch to back down, to say, okay, Mother, you're right, and call the marriage off. When that didn't happen, when Dutch just sat there, still holding Gina's hand, still looking like a man who always knew his own mother was never in his corner, she left the room. Left it with a harrumph that could still be felt by the vibrations of her door slam.

Gina looked at Dutch, her heart breaking for him. But he seemed more determined than she had ever seen him before.

"Okay," he said. "Now we know what we're up against."

"Meaning?"

"Before the gates of hell can gather their minions for the onslaught, we had better get on with it." He turned to Gina. "You said you would marry me," he said. "But will you marry me today?"

Gina stared at him. "Even without your mother's blessing?"

"Especially without her blessing. Or anybody else's. I will not let them turn our life into their political football. This is about us. And tonight, when I lay my head on my pillow, I want my wife, not my girlfriend, not my fiancée, lying beside me."

Tears dropped from Gina's eyes. After this train wreck with his mother, she expected him to have second thoughts at least. He, instead, had stiffened his resolve. "Yes," she said. "I'll be honored to marry you today."

She had seriously doubted all along if this could be pulled off in a matter of hours. But he orchestrated the entire affair. And by the time they arrived at the White House, and up to the residence, the decorations were up, LaLa and Dempsey were waiting, the minister was there, Christian was there, and they were married.   Married as a firestorm of hate and objection gathered around them. Married as his mother issued her press release, condemning any relationship her son was having with Regina Lansing. Married as Kate waited for him to ask, under duress even she would admit, for her hand in marriage.

Despite it all, and because of it all, they became husband and wife. And that night, when they lay down to sleep, Dutch pulled the spanking brand new Mrs. Regina Harber into his arms, and held her, with tears in his eyes, all night long.

SEVENTEEN

At the daily presser in the briefing room, Max and Allison were reviewing the president's schedule for today and answering any questions the press might have. Of course, most of the questions centered around the statement issued by Victoria Harber disavowing the president's relationship with Regina Lansing. Although the statement didn't mention the marriage proposal, since it was not yet public, it was still enough of a slap in the president's face to make what Max called the media hounds bloodthirsty.

But before any definitive answer could be given, other than the obligatory *the president was disappointed with his mother's decision not to be supportive of him*, the president himself, along with Gina, came into the briefing room.

The entire audience of reporters and White House correspondents stood to their feet in pleased surprise.

"Please, be seated," Dutch said as he and Gina stood at the podium.

Max and Allison, just as surprised by his appearance as the press, stood back, both deeply concerned because Regina was with him.

"I have a brief announcement," Dutch continued, pulling out an index card from his coat lapel. "Regina Lansing and I were married last night at the White House residence."

The gasps of shock that filled the room were so loud and so contagious that it sounded almost like high-voltage firecrackers had just gone off. Nobody saw this coming. Not even Max and Allison, who had not been told of the proposal, let alone told that they were already married. And although they were stunned beyond belief, they were political pros and looked out at the amazed press with stoic faces.

"In Regina," Dutch continued, "America will find a first lady who is smart, industrious, and with a heart of gold. She's a fighter and champion of the poor and disenfranchised and I am so honored, so unbelievably proud to have her as my wife. The love of my life. Thank-you, and have a nice day."

Dutch and Regina left the podium. No looks at Max and Allison, no responses to the myriad of questions the press stood and threw their way, with the dominant questions centering almost exclusively on how this marriage would affect his reelection campaign.

That was the question on Kate's mind, too, as she saw a rerun of the statement. And although she was devastated that her plan had blown up in her face, she held her own press conference, later that evening, where she announced to the world that she was pregnant with Dutch Harber's baby. And although he claims to be a family values president, she went on, he would not even marry her. That was why they broke up three months ago, she lied to the press, because she had told him she was pregnant, and he had told her to take a hike.

It was a lie, a bald-faced lie, but that same lie went viral. From YouTube to Facebook to Twitter to good old fashioned newscasts, the talk of the town was all about how Dutch Harber, family values president, was about to become a deadbeat dad.

It dominated the cable news channels that night. Dutch and Gina lay in bed watching them, flipping through channel after channel, and the commentary was all negative. No-one, not even members of the Congressional Black Caucus, who were often able to see a silver lining in the ways of their hero Dutch Harber, could see no positives in this.

"It's over," David Kirlings, a well-respected commentator for MSNBC, put it bluntly. "America is a forgiving country. And they like their president. But for Dutch Harber to dump Kate Marris because she became pregnant, is unconscionable. And yes, I know Max Brennan has been all over the airwaves beating back that assertion, saying it isn't true and that Dutch only found out about this pregnancy a few nights ago. But it still looks bad. And in Washington, how it looks matter a whole lot more than the reality of the thing. No, I'm afraid Dutch Harber is dead. He's done. There is no way he can overcome this and get reelected."

Dutch clicked off the television set and wrapped his arms around Gina. They were now on their sides, facing each other. "Put a fork in me, babe," he said jokingly, "because I'm done."

Gina stared into his eyes, refusing to minimize what she knew had to be very painful for him. "You can't resign," she said.

"Oh, I won't. I won't give Kate and her groupies that satisfaction. I'll see it to the end."

"Can you pull it out?" she asked him.

"In a word, no. David Kirlings right. But damn if I'm not going down without a fight. They can have this presidency, it's not mine anyway, it's the American people's, but they will have to take it from me."

Gina smiled. She loved his toughness. Almost as much as she loved him.

She put her hand on the side of his face. He was drained, she was drained. Everything had been such a battle for them. "I love you," she said to her husband.

"I love you more," he said to his wife, his face smiling a smile of weariness and expectation.

"That's what you think," she said, as she moved on top of his naked body. She kissed him so passionately in the mouth that he wrapped his arms around her and stopped her progression, stopped her from doing anything else but lay there and kiss him, his tongue exploring hers with the kind of urgency that belied his drain.

When he finally allowed her to come back up for air, she turned her own naked body around, until her back was to his face, until her ass was on his chest, and she leaned forward, to his engorged penis that was already long and thick and at her attention. And she took it in full into her mouth, licking and teasing it, smelling the sweet scent of the silk that sprang ever so slightly from it.

He squeezed and kissed her ass that sat like two gorgeous, tight cheeks in front of him. He kissed her cheeks, sucked and bit her cheeks, and opened her up to suck and lick her vagina. Her body reacted immediately when his tongue found her clit, and he flicked on it so much that she almost came in his face.

And when he began to groan, and expand even more in her own mouth, she knew it was time. And he took over then, lying her back onto his stomach and lifting her up, her legs in the air, as he began sliding his penis into her, sliding it in as if it was going through a tunnel so familiar, so relaxing that it kept teasing, kept sliding in and out, out and in, until the feeling became too intense to tease.

He spread her legs apart and rammed further and further into her, lifting her up and down on his penis, as he moved in deeper and deeper with every lift up, until he was pounding her, flesh pounding against flesh in the quietness of their room.

He became so engorged that he released into her with a splash that made him even more excited, that made him pound her even harder, the slime sliding out and slapping against her ass, until her body arched too high, because she couldn't bear the intensity of the feeling any longer, and he arched higher, to keep pounding her.

Until finally she arched too high for him to reach. And they both fell back down.

And just like that, as she continued to lay on top of him, as he wrapped her into his arms and wanted to cry with the joy and love he felt for this special lady, all of the chatter and doomsday

scenarios that clogged up every inch of
Washington discussions, meant nothing more to
them than other people's problems.

EPILOGUE

The election was called early, at exactly nine-twenty-two pm. And it was no contest. The winner was cocky with elation and the loser, more subdued, had to face his supporters, too.

The crowds began to swell now, from one-two-three hundred to thousands was now the estimate, as their loyalty for Dutch Harber, the embattled president, became more and more evident. Many of his supporters felt that he had gotten a rotten deal ever since that Kate Marris pregnancy story broke. And even after her unfortunate miscarriage, the media still wouldn't let up, pouncing on Dutch for not giving his condolences in person. But what was the man to do? She had lied on him, lied in an orchestrated attempt to bring his presidency down, and he was supposed to just overlook that fact and feel sorry for her?

That was why his supporters felt as if he had been treated unfairly beyond belief, while his opponent, Kentucky Governor Ray Branchett, had gotten a free ride. No digging into his dubious land deals and questionable business practices before he became Governor of Kentucky. Nothing but praise and more praise for him.

But the crowds kept coming, right there on the south lawn of the White House. No major convention hall had been booked because it seemed wholly unnecessary. Only the faithful few would show up at the loser's concession speech, was the theory.

But tonight was different. Electricity was in the air. And when the announcement came, the silence was penetrable.

"Ladies and gentlemen, after a year-long contest that tried the souls of man, we are pleased to present the man who ran an honest campaign, who refused to bow down to special interests groups and so-called friends who advised him to go negative and stay negative. He stayed positive. And tonight, the American people have spoken and have made clear that they want a positive leader, that they want hope over fear, that they want character over bravado. Ladies and gentlemen, please welcome the newly reelected President of the United States, Walter "Dutch" Harber, and still first lady, Regina Harber!"

The crowd went wild as Dutch and Gina made their way to the makeshift stage. It was all thrown together last minute, when exit polling began to break their way. The pollsters were saying no, Dutch didn't stand a chance, but somehow, to the delight of Dutch and Gina, the pollsters proved wrong.

Dutch couldn't stop grinning as he and Gina waved and waved to a crowd that was nearly delirious with happiness. He took a moment and looked at Gina, who could not have looked more radiant to him.

"We actually pulled this off," he said with a grin only the Cheshire Cat could top.

"Thank God," she said, more relieved than he would ever know.

Their love became their tonic as they clasped hands and pumped their fists in the kind of triumphant jubilation only those who have come back from the brink could feel.

Gina couldn't stop grinning, because she knew what the brink looked like. Everybody said they weren't going to make it. Everybody said a woman like her would drag a man like him down. Everybody said everything negative they could fix their venomous mouths to say. But God, Gina thought, as she stared proudly at her victorious husband, said different.

ABOUT THE AUTHOR

Mallory Monroe is the bestselling author of numerous novels, including Mob Boss 2: The Heart of the Matter, Romancing the Mob Boss, Romancing Her Protector, Romancing the Bulldog, and If You Wanted the Moon.

Visit www.austinbrookpublishing.com for more information on all of her titles.

Made in the USA
San Bernardino, CA
12 December 2012